"Your play," Carl Lyons told him

David McCarter walked to the warehouse door and pushed it open.

Even after the darkness of the dockside the interior was dim. Three forty-watt bulbs in small reflectors hung overhead, silhouetting the four men who sat on bar stools along a counter.

"We're looking for Helen," McCarter said without moving any closer.

Slowly one of the men turned and stood. He was well over six feet tall and easily weighed more than three hundred pounds—it was all solid muscle.

"It's Mr. Helen to you. What the hell do you want?"

"Guns."

"You're already carrying."

"I'm told you can supply them by the hundreds."

"You were told wrong."

McCarter turned to confer with Lyons. A sinking feeling in the pit of his stomach told him that Able Team had been double-crossed.

As if on cue, a group of men emerged from the shadows. Each was armed with an M-16 and each found a target.

Mack Bolan's

ABLE TEAM

ABLE TEAM

FIRECROSS

Dick Stivers

A GOLD EAGLE BOOK FROM
WORLDWIDE

TORONTO • NEW YORK • LONDON • PARIS
AMSTERDAM • STOCKHOLM • HAMBURG
ATHENS • MILAN • TOKYO • SYDNEY

First edition October 1987

ISBN 0-373-61232-X

Special thanks and acknowledgment to
Tom Arnett for his contribution to this work.

Printed in Canada

PROLOGUE

The voice at the other end of the telephone conversation chilled Francis Overton, president of Megatronics Ltd., the manufacturer of LSIs—large-scale integrated chips.

"Overton, Megatronics is wired with five remote-controlled bombs. They will be set off one at a time unless you do exactly as told."

"Is this a joke?" Overton asked. The knot in the pit of his stomach told him that it wasn't.

"Look in your lower right-hand desk drawer, the one you always keep locked," the flat, rasping voice directed.

"Just a moment," Overton replied. As he fished for his keys, his knee pressed a button under his desk, sending an emergency signal to both his secretary and to plant security.

The person on the other end of the telephone whistled loudly, attracting the executive's attention.

"That was naughty," the voice told him. "I did not tell you to press your hidden button. You must be taught a lesson. Look in the drawer. Wait until you are told about the extent of the bomb's damage. Then I will call you back."

The line went dead and then the sound of an explosion rocked the building. Overton's secretary threw open the door to his office, standing clear as she'd been instructed to do if ever summoned by the emergency buzzer.

"What's happening? Was that an explosion? Are we under attack?" she called through the open door, her voice reflecting her panic.

"I want a full report on the blast immediately. Then I want a bomb expert to open my desk drawer," Overton barked.

No one in England questioned the word "bomb"; the British were used to acts of terrorism. She moved to her telephone and carried out his instructions.

A police inspector arrived at Overton's office at the same time as Norton, Megatronics's chief of security. Norton managed to get in the first word.

"It was my car. Not much left of it, nor the cars on either side."

"Anyone hurt?" Overton asked, more shaken than he let on. He hadn't failed to miss the significance of the terrorist's target.

"Doesn't seem to be, sir," the police inspector said.

"I want a bomb expert to open my desk drawer," Overton told him. "I just had a telephone call telling me to look in there."

"Clear the building, sir. The bomb squad is on its way. They'll tend to it immediately."

Overton left his office to help speed the evacuation of the plant. Determined-looking police officers wearing padded vests pushed past him toward his office.

Minutes later, the only people in or near Megatronics were Overton, the company's security staff and the police. Overton was summoned back into his office.

"Nothing dangerous in here, sir," the inspector reported. "Just some liquor and this. I'll have to ask you not to touch it, sir. We'll want to check it for prints."

The note, spread out on Overton's black walnut desk, was printed on cheap stationery with a soft pencil. "There are four more bombs on the premises," it read.

Francis Overton stared at the note, entranced by the horror of its message. Then he was roused by the ringing of his private telephone. He picked it up, still staring at the note.

"You have two choices," the rasping voice told him. "You can deliver a dozen chips, the laser scanning prints for making them and fifty thousand pounds where I tell you. Or you and the police can attempt to defuse the bombs faster than I can trigger them."

"I can't get those things together in time," the Megatronics president said in a flat voice.

"You can have all the time you want," the terrorist assured him. The voice rattled with self-satisfaction. "I want everyone out of the building except yourself. You stay. We counted the police going in. We shall count them going out. We know Norton's men. If everyone is out in five minutes, no one will start pushing buttons.

"When we see a bank messenger deliver the money, you will be told what to do next. When the money is delivered, you will be told where to find the bombs and how to disarm them."

The line went dead.

Overton looked up. The policeman's ear was one inch from his own. The inspector had heard the entire conversation.

"There's one other choice," the inspector said. "We can all walk out of here in five minutes."

Overton shook his head. With one competitor, Megatronics could stay in business. Besides, they could use a court injunction to shut down anyone who tried manufacturing their chip. The important thing was to get the bombs out of the factory. Fifty thousand pounds was a blow, but it wouldn't bankrupt them.

"We pay."

MANIFRED EDWARDS, president of Gammabase Delta, opened the door to his Bentley and got out of the car. His two bodyguards were already standing on the street side of the car, watching for trouble.

Edwards, tall, gray-haired and dignified, glanced around uneasily. His strong views against those who tried to subvert democracy with violence were well-known. To prove how wrong the industrialist was the IRA had tried several times to kill him.

The heavy morning traffic had let up one hour ago. The noon-hour rush of office workers and those who'd come into Birmingham to shop had not yet begun. The road wasn't busy, and the sidewalk was deserted because a work crew was tearing it up within ten feet of the entrance to Gammabase Delta. He sighed and straightened his shoulders.

Edwards had taken only a couple of paces when each of his bodyguards found a Colt 1911A1 held to his head. Two men in coveralls closed in on Edwards. One held an Ingram MAC-11, the other a Colt. The American weapons didn't surprise the Englishman. The IRA supplied most of the terrorist cells and many of the criminals in Britain. And the United States supplied the IRA.

"No trouble," one of the "workers" growled. "Relax and no one gets hurt." There was no trace of Irish in the terrorist's accent.

The bodyguards were quickly stripped of their bulky Beretta 84s.

"Back in the car," someone directed Edwards, who promptly followed instructions.

The two guards were viciously pistol-whipped. The terrorists jumped into the Bentley, and the car sped around the corner. There, everyone transferred to a small moving van, three captors accompanying Edwards into the back of the truck.

William Younger, senior vice president of Gammabase Delta, took command as soon as it became evident that the president of the firm had been kidnapped. The two bodyguards had been rushed to hospital. One was not expected to live; both were still unconscious.

The call came through almost two hours after Edwards had been kidnapped.

"Yes?" Younger asked cautiously.

"Who is this?" the voice demanded.

"What do you want?" the senior vice president countered.

"You must be Younger," the rough voice decided. "You are the only asshole who would play games while the ship sank."

Younger winced and couldn't prevent himself from glancing at the man who sat on the other side of his office, listening on an extension. The man grinned, indicating he agreed with the terrorist's assessment. Younger wished he could fire the son of a bitch.

The listener was extremely tall—six foot five, Younger guessed. He dressed well, but not excessively so. He had a long horselike face that ended in a lantern jaw. Younger placed him at forty, certainly no older than that. Van Nice had good credentials, but Younger wished someone else had been available. The counterterrorism specialist was expensive, and he'd laughed in Younger's face when the vice president had tried to get him to accept a lower fee. But Quinton Van Nice was the only industrial agent experienced with this type of threat.

"I'm Younger," the senior vice president admitted. "What do you want?"

"One hundred thousand pounds and the manufacturing specifications for the Gamma bubble drive," the voice demanded.

"Hardly..." Younger began. He paused when he saw Van Nice signaling him to say yes.

"Hardly any choice," the gravel voice said. The amusement in the voice stung Younger.

"What do you mean?" Younger asked. It was an inane question, but he wanted to stall while he read the note passed to him by Van Nice.

"Don't try to stall me," the voice warned him. "I am not noted for my patience."

It was long enough for Younger to read, "Don't haggle price. Haggle guarantees of Edwards's safety."

"It'll take time to raise that much," Younger said. His voice quivered as he fought to suppress his temper. "Don't haggle price" was all right for Van Nice to say. He didn't have to answer to the directors.

"You have twenty-four hours. After that we ship Edwards back to you a piece at a time."

Something about the matter-of-fact tone of the voice told Younger the speaker meant exactly what she said. He shivered.

"How do we know Mr. Edwards is all right?"

"You don't."

"I'm not buying dead meat," Younger shot back. There was genuine anger in his voice. He'd been company comptroller before being promoted to vice president. He wouldn't spend money without benefit.

"You will see him before you pass over the money and the plans," the gravel voice conceded. "Small, nonconsecutive bills, unmarked. Put the money and the plans into a shopping bag."

"A what?"

"A carrier bag, idiot. And no police. We are watching you. Go to the police, and Edwards dies, painfully. I shall phone again with delivery instructions."

The line went dead.

"American," Younger said with distaste as he hung up the telephone.

"Probably a non-English-speaking person who learned English in the United States," Van Nice said.

Younger didn't appreciate being corrected.

"What makes you say that?"

"Very few contractions in her speech. Americans can spend years here and still not know what a carrier bag is."

Younger shrugged. "What now?"

"Get the money and plans together. I'll make arrangements to cover the exchange."

"You don't really expect me to give those...those terrorists what they're asking for?"

"You're calling the shots, but it's considered advisable to get your executive back before you move in to retrieve the ransom. Otherwise, you'll likely have a dead president on your hands."

Younger knew he was trapped. The board would never let him step into the president's chair if he hadn't done everything possible to save Edwards.

"We'll do it your way," he told Van Nice. His tone of voice added that if anything went wrong, Van Nice would bear the responsibility.

"HELL OF A TIME to make a delivery," Quinton Van Nice muttered under his breath. "A freezing, ruddy Saturday afternoon."

He sat hunched miserably on the plank seat of a narrowboat, watching the countryside creep by. The forty-four-foot-long, seven-foot-wide boat putted along the narrow waterway at the rate of five miles an hour. Half a dozen tourists huddled closer to the stern so that they could hear the heavily accented spiel delivered by the one-man captain, crew and tour guide.

The network of canals scattered through the central and southern half of England was becoming very popular with tourists. Van Nice knew the tour boats were converted coal vessels that were once pulled through the canals by horses. They had been cleaned up, brightly painted and now used small inboards to ply the waterways with much more lucrative loads of tourists.

The cruise he'd been instructed to take left Birmingham's Gas Street Basin and coughed and choked its way south to Stratford-upon-Avon—a twenty-two-mile trip that took four hours and twenty minutes on the narrowboat. Van Nice knew exactly how long it took, because he'd made the trip once already. He looked at the paper bag with rope handles that sat at his feet, and snorted.

Inside the bag, wrapped in newspapers as if it were fish and chips, were a hundred thousand pounds and a small manual of manufacturing specifications. The industrial terrorism expert shifted the bag, careful not to get it wet. All he needed now was for a wet bag to break and dump its contents into the canal.

He'd caught the 8:30 trip as the terrorist had instructed and had ridden the entire way to Stratford without being accosted. He hadn't bothered to watch for his agents, since he knew they would be covering his movements from the land. He was wired for sound and had men waiting to follow whoever picked up the bag. But no one had shown up to be followed.

Van Nice had expected little more. It was sensible procedure to miss the first drop in order to observe the messenger boy. It was a good way to see who was keeping the payment in sight. When he'd stepped off the narrowboat in Stratford, a small boy had handed him a note. It had told him to take the boat back again. That had puzzled Van Nice. Usually he was told to take another route back to make it easier to separate him from whatever cover he had.

He'd had a quick, tasteless lunch and caught the same boat back to Birmingham. They were within an hour of reaching the city and still no one had approached him. He'd casually checked at road crossings and was reassured that his men were covering his return trip. He was thankful he had competent men.

Then, when they passed under a small footbridge, a stone with a note tied to it dropped at his feet. Van Nice looked back but couldn't see anyone on the bridge, not even one of his own men. His men should have been covering every overpass.

He picked up the stone, untied the note and tossed the rock overboard. The instructions were simple: "Edwards will be a passenger in the next boat that passes. After you see him, place the bag on the hook hanging from the next bridge."

It was a good way to show that the victim was alive without much risk. No one would be able to tell how many of the people surrounding the president of Gammabase Delta were kidnappers and how many were innocent tourists. Van Nice was a professional, and he appreciated the professional skills being demonstrated by the other side.

Another narrowboat, going the other way, passed them in the canal. Both boats had to slow down because the channel was so narrow. Sitting in the middle seat, surrounded by grim-faced men and women, was a gray-haired man who matched perfectly the description of Manifred Edwards. He raised his trilby, uncovering the bald spot Van Nice had been told to watch for. Van Nice admired the president's cool way of confirming identification—a very different man from the sour vice president.

The next bridge was just ahead. The hook was easily visible. Van Nice simply raised the bag by its sides and let the hook catch the handles. The skipper of the small craft stopped in midspiel, and the tourists gaped as they passed under the bag, already being pulled to the bridge.

Van Nice glanced back quickly but saw no sign of his own men. That was how it should be. They weren't supposed to close in until they were sure Edwards had been released. Van Nice faced front, anxious for the ride to be over so that he could take command. He didn't dare give the game away by not riding out the last twenty minutes of the return trip.

The boat approached two other bridges, first a small footbridge, then a larger car bridge. They were on the outskirts of Birmingham. Another note, tied to a stone, dropped at Van Nice's feet. Aware of the burning curiosity of his fellow passengers, the tall man stooped and snatched up the stone, yanking off the note.

"The manual isn't genuine," the hasty scrawl read.

Van Nice was still cursing Younger's double-dealing when the grenade landed from the next bridge. He had only time to register what was happening before the grenade blew him to pieces.

URIEL ISAAC, chairman of the board of Quartermaster Software Incorporated, had been at his desk for ten hours. He'd cleared his in-tray and had been given a capsule briefing on company activities by Nate Zimmerman, the CEO.

He reminded himself that it hadn't really been ten hours. He had arrived at his desk at five, as he usually did on the two days a week he came into work, but he'd taken two hours for lunch.

He smiled at that thought. During those two hours, he'd had tea and chatted with the assembly workers and technicians over the span of both lunch breaks. Many of the employees were delighted to "have a spot with the old skipper." He didn't gain specific information from his occasional forays into the staff dining room, but he did keep a trained finger on the emotional pulse of the production line. He was proud of the healthy attitudes he found there.

The London-based company was doing amazingly well. Isaac hadn't been sure of its future when he had kicked himself upstairs and turned the company over to the employees. But he had no heir and couldn't stand to simply sell the company he'd taken twenty years to build.

Isaac remained the largest stockholder, hanging on to thirty percent of the shares. He was an active chairman of the board, coming in twice a week to be briefed and to perform those functions best handled through personal contact with other businesses. Many people still couldn't think of Quartermaster Software without thinking of Uriel Isaac.

He pushed back from his desk and thought about that. His old acquaintances *would* do business with Nate; they simply preferred to keep up familiar contacts. Nate was doing brilliantly. The software being developed for Megatronics's new chip would double Quartermaster's size in the next two years. Isaac was beginning to feel like an old warhorse, hanging on past his time.

His thoughts were interrupted by the ringing of his telephone. He picked it up, happy to switch his mind to other channels.

"Isaac here."

The voice on the other side was raspy and devoid of inflection. "Do you know what happened to Edwards?"

"He was stabbed and dumped in a canal by terrorists. Is this a threat?" Isaac asked as his finger pushed a button that would put an automatic trace on the call. The device wasn't exactly illegal, but it would be if legislators knew it existed.

"Not to you. But it could happen to your employees, one at a time." The cold and expressionless voice added a new dimension of horror to the words.

"And what do you expect me to do while you conduct this systematic slaughter?" For a small man, Isaac had a deep, commanding voice. There was no suggestion in it of the cold hand he now felt squeezing his heart.

His question was ignored. "Soon you will demand to know what I want. Then you will tell me that I will never get away with this." Contemptuous humor sneered at him from her words.

"I know what you want. You have Megatronics's new chip, but you lack the intelligence to develop your own programming software to complement it."

"That comment will cost you one employee. Have you any more insults?"

"No."

Isaac was kicking himself. What had he done? Who would pay for his failure to control the contempt he felt for all criminal terrorists?

"I want copies of all the work disks, plus the source codes for the software. Protect the disks well and wrap them, along with one hundred thousand pounds, in a brown paper package. I will let you know when and where to deliver it."

"That will take weeks."

"If you take that long, several will die. You have three days. Someone will call you with delivery instructions."

The line went dead.

Isaac glanced at his call tracer. It had registered a phone number. He rang for the secretary assigned to him on the days he came into the office.

The door opened, and an exceptionally beautiful young woman walked into the room. She was extremely efficient, but Isaac had to admit he missed the battle-ax who'd retired when he'd moved himself upstairs.

"Miss Jones, please ask Mr. Zimmerman to come in right away. Tell him it's urgent. Then I want you to put a call through to Minneapolis for me, to Able Group."

When she looked puzzled, he paused, then looked in his address file.

"Here it is. Toni Blancanales of Able Group. Get the call through quickly, please."

She nodded, accepted the proffered card and withdrew.

Isaac sat stiffly upright, impatiently waiting for things to happen. They'd been paying Able Group a healthy retainer for years. It was the best industrial security company in the States, and the time had come for it to earn its fee.

1

Toni Blancanales checked over the final details on the presentation she planned to make that afternoon. It would be a large contract, and the proposal had been carefully researched. She had sold the company's management on it, and now she had to convince their board of directors.

She leaned back against the leather of her high-backed desk chair and looked out past her teak desk at the Minneapolis skyline. From her office on the thirty-fourth floor of the Downtown Center, she could see for miles—skyscrapers, and then off in the distance, the gray, bare trees waiting for the first winter snows.

The two senior partners of Able Group were now merely figureheads who spent most of their time at Stony Man Farm. They were part of the President's antiterrorist force—a team that fought terrorism directed at the United States. Their role was invaluable, but it left Toni with the entire executive responsibility for the industrial security firm. She often met the stresses of high-pressure management by losing herself for a few minutes in the serene view from her office window.

When her telephone rang, she picked up the white handset, but most of her mind was still reviewing the proposal. The crisp British voice on the other end cut through her thoughts.

"Uriel Isaac here. Toni, we've got problems."

Toni pulled herself upright, the proposal forgotten.

"Shoot."

Isaac quickly summarized his situation and filled Toni in on the raids on Megatronics and Gammabase Delta. Toni's mind did a quick scan of staff. Who was free to go with her? Who was up to handling a problem like this one?

"Move slowly, Uriel, but give them what they want. I'll get there with a team as quickly as I can. We'll take over negotiations and delivery as soon as we arrive, but the important thing is to keep your people breathing."

"The important thing is to keep the business functioning," Isaac snapped, the tension showing for the first time.

"The business is no good to dead men," Toni said as gently as she could. "Avoid a hard line until I'm there to take the brunt of it. That's what you pay us for."

"I pay you to keep us out of messes like this," he barked.

"We never promised that. We told you we could reduce the likelihood, but no one can stop terrorists from choosing a particular target."

A heavy sigh sounded in her ear. "I know. It's just that I hate feeling so helpless."

"Hang on. Don't take any risks."

"When will you be here?"

"I'll let you know as soon as I'm organized."

"Do that. I'll stay in the office until I hear from you. Nate's here now. I must brief him." Isaac hung up without saying goodbye.

Toni sat quietly and thought. This was going to be a tough one. Most of her staff were already handling other assignments. It was also a contract she couldn't afford to lose. The reputation of the firm would ride on her success against these terrorists. But could she do it alone? Toni picked up the phone and started dialing.

"DIE!" CARL LYONS SHOUTED as Babette's fist crashed into his solar plexus.

She stepped to one side, allowing Politician to throw a long, low jab to the same region.

"Die!" Lyons shouted with ear-splitting volume.

Politician took his place several feet from Babette while Lao Ti delivered her best roundhouse kick to the Ironman's midsection.

"Die!" he shouted as the ball of her foot crashed into his stomach, knocking him back two steps.

Lao went to stand beside Babette while Gadgets gave the Ironman a rapid one-two to the midsection.

"Die!" Lyons screamed again as the first punch hammered his bruised stomach area.

Gadgets moved between Politician and Lao while Lyons caught his wind.

"You see," said the deep, vibrant voice. "When you shout just before impact, the diaphragm is already on its way in. Then holding back the rest of your breath keeps the stomach muscles toned and dissipates much of the force of the blow. You must learn to use your lungs and your vocal cords when you fight. All your power comes from your *ki*. Now sit."

Still breathing hard, Carl Lyons sat cross-legged, staring at the four people standing ten feet in front of him. He was aware that Kekupa'a stood behind him, but Lyons tuned out the awareness, except for the deep bell-like voice. The four people before him were relaxed, yet ready to take instant action. Lyons studied each one as he let the words of the Hawaiian *lua* master reverberate in his head.

Rosario Blancanales stood on the left. Politician to the other members of Able Team, he stood five foot eleven, erect, poised. He had white wavy hair and black eyes. At the moment he wore nothing but sweatpants. But even dressed so casually, there was something dignified about the man, and something in the dark eyes that spoke both of suffering and understanding. Lyons could see clearly why the image Politician presented made him highly approachable and easy to get along with.

People would find it hard to guess Blancanales's age. The white hair made him look like a statesman of about fifty-five. The tanned, hard, bullet-scarred body belonged to a man of twenty-nine. Lyons knew his friend was somewhere in between.

"You should see four of them," the voice from behind Lyons continued, "but you should be aware that each person standing before you has two natures: the animal being that any other animal can see and the spiritual being or presence that the warrior must learn to see. Look at them until you see both aspects of all four."

Next to Politician stood Hermann "Gadgets" Schwarz, undisciplined electronics genius, penetration expert and all-around wiseass. He stood five foot ten and weighed in ten pounds lighter than his teammate. Gadgets's hair was brown and was worn longer than Politician's. He sported a bushy mustache that, for some reason, accented the humor that was forever lurking in his soft brown eyes. Even now, Gadgets's mouth twitched minutely at the left corner.

He's even more cynical than I am, Lyons thought to himself. The realization shocked him.

Kekupa'a's voice brought Lyons back to the exercise. "Pay attention! Just because you do not understand a thing does not mean that thing has no existence. Focus on these beings until you see their mana, their spiritual power."

Lyons brought his attention back and focused on his friends. Kekupa'a had saved his life once when he had overextended himself in the Ironman Triathlon. The *lua* exercises didn't make sense to Lyons, but he had to admit he'd recovered quickly from being beyond the point of mental and physical exhaustion. He'd do his best to please the Hawaiian master.

Standing next in line was Lao Ti. Lao had often helped Able Team in the past, although she held down a job as an electrical engineer. Her training in the martial arts gave her an advantage over many of her enemies. She spent as much time at the Farm, or on training sessions with the team, as her job allowed.

Lao often helped to program Stony Man's computer. She didn't quite have Gadgets's ability to put together a radio or a bug from the unlikeliest pieces of scrap, but she had prevented Able Team from being handicapped by computer-wielding killers.

Yeah, Lyons decided in the silence of his soul. She's one of us. She even looks like one of us.

Lyons was barely aware that the voice behind him, the deep, ringing voice, had stopped. He shifted his eyes to the fourth person standing in front of him.

Babette Pavlovski wasn't a member of the team. She was a great gymnast, a mean fighter and someone special to Gadgets. Her form was compatible with Able Team's, not identical.

Only then did the absurdity of Lyons's thoughts penetrate his consciousness. Lao looked like the rest of Able Team! Tiny, female Lao Ti and three hulking men? Then Lyons realized he was seeing those in front of him not as people but as forces. That small package did indeed contain a force equal to the others and identical in its craving for justice.

"He understands," Kekupa'a told the four.

"Sure. He understands we're tired of standing around," Gadgets shot back.

"You will see," the instructor answered. Then he told Lyons, "Stand up and turn your back on them."

A young student of Kekupa'a ran to the *lua* master and whispered in his ear.

"I will tell them later. Wait," the deep, ringing voice instructed the pupil.

"You four are to jump your friend and take him to the ground," Kekupa'a said. "And you, Lyons, must evade them without turning around."

Lyons nodded. Maybe once he'd been pinned to the ground they could break off this training session and go for breakfast. He was hungry.

They stood in a clearing surrounded by palms. The sand made little noise under their bare feet, and what sound it did make was drowned by the roar of the Pacific as large breakers rolled onto the beach fifty yards away. Dawn had broken, but the sun was still lounging below the horizon.

Gadgets, the most practiced at moving silently, vaulted across the sand to tackle Lyons before he was set. Lyons moved to one side, and Gadgets ended up with an armful of cold sand.

Babette tried a spring to plant both feet in Lyons's back. He flexed his knees, letting her legs slide over his left shoulder. Then he straightened and dumped her on her back.

Lyons followed that by an immediate move to the right to avoid Pol's kick to the back of his leg.

Lao crept up to him slowly and then threw herself at his ankles, her arms wide in an attempt to gather in his legs whichever way he stepped. He leaped in the air and came down with a foot on either side of her back as she sprawled in the sand. Lyons could have snapped her spine if he'd simply kept his feet together.

Gadgets tried a side kick, only to have his foot brushed away. Lyons had still not turned to face his assailants.

The gymnast, Babette, leaped high into the air in an attempt to come down on the Ironman's shoulders. She almost succeeded. At the last moment he took a step forward, and she brushed past, unable to knock him over.

At a signal from Gadgets, both he and Politician made flying tackles from opposite sides while Lao charged right up the center. Lyons tried to fake them out but couldn't avoid all three. He went down in a puff of sand.

"Enough," Kekupa'a told them. "There is a long-distance call for both Mr. Blancanales and Mr. Schwarz. My young friend tells me it is urgent."

Pol and Gadgets took off with the student as a guide. Kekupa'a signaled for the two women to leave. Then he sat down on his haunches facing Lyons. Lyons straightened up and sat facing the tall Hawaiian.

"You will be leaving soon," the Hawaiian said.

"The phone call?"

"I suspect something urgent has arisen. I sense you and your friends are familiar with such urgent requests."

"What happened just then?" Lyons asked in an attempt to change the subject. "Why did it take four people so long to bowl me over?"

"You avoided them."

"How? I wasn't looking. And don't give me that god-to-god jazz."

Kekupa'a smiled. "It is my culture's way of expressing it. Call it chi if you are Chinese."

"And if I'm from good old nonsuperstitious U.S. of A.?"

"Then call it subliminal impression, although I admit that even I am not superstitious enough to believe in perceiving things too slight to be perceived. It does not matter what you call it."

"But I don't believe that stuff."

"You do not have to believe the law of gravity either, but what happens to you when you step off a high cliff?"

"You make it sound so...so natural."

"I do not believe in the supernatural."

"What! With all your talk of gods?"

"You are a man and a god. So am I. So are your friends. That is not supernatural. That is natural."

Lyons shook his head. "I'll keep trying, but I have a feeling I wasn't meant to understand."

"You do understand. You do not want to admit you understand. But you will not try again. The telephone call means someone is in urgent need of help."

Lyons looked up to see Politician running across the sand toward him. "Gadgets and I have an emer—" He broke off as Kekupa'a rose to his feet.

Kekupa'a bowed to them. Lyons scrambled to his feet, and both men returned the bow. The towering Hawaiian left without another word or sign.

"That was Toni," Pol explained. "One of Able Group's clients is having terrorist troubles in Britain. Gadgets and I feel we should go if we're not needed at the Farm."

"Let's take Babette along. I'm sure she'll want to come," Lyons said. There was a crispness to his voice that had been absent a few seconds earlier.

"How do you know?"

"She's that kind of friend," Lyons snapped. "Better book us on a commercial flight, then get back to Toni. It'll be faster to take a regular airline than to wait for Stony Man to send something to pick us up. Faster and safer. That way no one else has tabs on our arrival."

The six-foot-two blond warrior strode toward the pounding ocean, intent on a swim. Politician had to follow to continue the discussion.

"We'll never get our weapons onto a commercial flight. Not with all these new safety precautions."

"We'll leave everything except our clothes, the flak jackets, Gadgets's tech gear and your *jo* with Kekupa'a. We'll pick up weapons and heavier clothing there."

"I don't like it."

Lyons turned his ice-blue eyes on Blancanales. "You could always wait for Stony Man to clear a flight with the British government. That is, if they'd do it. We're still on R and R. This isn't official government business, and if it was, the President might not want us in on it. We're only sanctioned to protect American interests *in* the U.S."

"I don't like that, either. Okay, I'll book us on the first available flight."

Lyons didn't bother acknowledging. He strode into the breaking surf and struck out as if he intended to swim to the mainland.

THE SUN WAS BRIGHT for London. It shone in the window behind Aya Jishin, making it difficult to discern her features. She sat at a scarred metal desk in a ten-by-twelve-foot rented office. She was a short, wide, flat-faced Japanese woman with the cold heart of a crocodile.

A short tap on the flimsy door broke her concentration. Jishin's response sounded like the snarl of a hunting cat.

The man who entered was five foot ten and broad enough to fill the doorway. His head was covered by black and gray fuzz, none of it longer than a quarter inch. His hands, like Jishin's, were deformed by the hard style of karate that they both practiced. He closed the door on the dingy hallway.

Squinting against the light, he reported, "The woman in Minneapolis telephoned Quartermaster. She and other members of her firm will be arriving at Heathrow at 5:40 tomorrow morning."

Jishin's flat face split into a gap-toothed grin.

"Considerate of them to be so prompt. I need not leave for the United States until later in the day. Have that red-headed English bastard, the photographer, at Heathrow. I want photographs of our enemies. Make sure he understands they are not to know their pictures are being taken."

"I gather from the orders Isaac telephoned to his chauffeur that he will be meeting them personally."

She paused, swung around to look at the back of the Quartermaster Software building, then growled, "I don't like it. We can monitor Isaac in his office and on the telephones. But while they travel from Heathrow, any plans they make will be lost to us."

"Maybe he should not reach the airport?" the assistant suggested.

Jishin thought about it. "Not bad, Yoru. Only let's wait until he is in the terminal. If we hold Isaac, his employees will give us whatever we want. If we grab him in front of his security specialists, no one will have any faith in their abilities. Do it."

Yoru bowed to signify the orders would be carried out. Aya Jishin wasn't ready to dismiss him.

She glanced over at the monitoring equipment and tape recorders piled in one corner of the tiny office.

"Have they finished transcribing yesterday's tapes?"

"Yes. Just the normal business we've been monitoring for the past week."

This caused the bulky Japanese woman to ponder for another moment. "That means he is putting all his faith in this American woman and her company. They must be very professional."

The stocky man bowed again, putting his closed fist into his open palm. "Maybe they should be eliminated?"

"Better to make them lose face. We must not be side-tracked. These raids in England are merely to get us started. Our main objectives are in the United States. We will cripple the entire American electronics industry. But first, we will trap and eliminate the group that disrupted my plans once before." Her voice was hard with anger.

As she spoke, her left hand grabbed the corner of the metal desk and curved it upward as if it were light tin.

Yoru opened his mouth to say something, but thought better of it. The yakuza had trained him, and he'd been offended when told he'd be second-in-command to a woman. But now that he'd met her, he admitted to himself that she was fearless. He bowed again and hurried from the room to carry out her orders. Yoru found himself hoping these Americans would get in his way. He yearned to vent his anger on someone.

THE FLIGHT FROM Hawaii to London stopped for an hour and a half in San Francisco to refuel. Toni had flown west from Minneapolis so she could be on the same flight and brief Able Team on the way.

Toni was even shorter than Lao Ti, but much more generously curved. Her eyes were big, and like her brother's, they were black. Her black hair was caught in a fashionable ponytail at the back of her head. Her gray business suit was both conservative and expensive, the perfect outfit for a British boardroom.

The widebody jet landed at Heathrow in an icy fog long before sunrise. On the moving sidewalk that took them from the plane into the terminal, the members of Able Team shivered in their tropical-weight suits.

"This climate's strictly glacialville," Gadgets complained. "Where are we going to get chem packs to warm our flak jackets? The packs we had with us in Hawaii only cool things down."

"Use one of those and imagine you're back on the beach," Politician suggested.

"Yeah. Wouldn't I be the cool gent. After you."

Even at that hour the airport was crowded and incredibly noisy. The myriad signs telling them where to go to find their baggage barely stood out in the forest of advertisements.

The six travelers scanned the crowd while they waited for their baggage to arrive from the plane.

"Who's supposed to meet us?" Gadgets asked.

"Someone from Quartermaster Software. I don't know who," Toni answered.

"Someone's watching us," Lyons said in a casual voice.

None of the team members looked around immediately. Lao dropped her flight bag and glanced around as she picked it up. Gadgets used the glass separating them from a passenger lounge to survey the crowd.

"Where?" Pol asked. He was leaning on the white oak cane that doubled as a *jo*, or short fighting stick.

Lyons swung around and swept his gaze over the crowd, not caring that he was obviously scanning faces. The rest of the team suddenly realized it was a perfectly natural action for someone who expected to be met at the plane.

"The redheaded man with the telephoto lens back near the escalators," Lyons reported.

"Shall we try to catch him?" Lao asked.

"Too hard in this crowd. He's on home turf. Let's pretend we couldn't care less."

"Somehow I get the feeling you really don't care," Gadgets remarked.

Before Lyons could reply, Toni suddenly waved her hand and called out, "Over here, Uriel."

The man who approached wasn't much taller than Toni. Age had turned his skin parchment yellow, but it hadn't added weight or stooped his shoulders. The impeccably dressed man removed his bowler when he saw Toni Blancanales, revealing a shiny bald pate surrounded by the merest fringe of white fluff.

As if the removal of the hat were a signal, three men closed in on him.

2

When Carl Lyons saw the men move in on Toni's friend, the Ironman naturally slipped into his habit of quick strategic thinking and lightning command.

"Gadgets, Lao, outflank. Watch for a backup squad. Hold position until needed. Politician, you and I go up the middle."

"Hey," Toni objected. "This is an Able Group operation."

No one paid her any attention. Lao and Schwarz faded into the crowd. Ironman and Politician bracketed Toni and moved past her toward Uriel Isaac.

Thugs had grabbed each of Isaac's wrists. Both men had used their left hand, leaving their right hands free. The one who held Isaac's left wrist stood partly behind his prisoner. Lyons and Politician both knew that the concealed right hand could be holding a weapon against the prisoner's back.

Neither of the two Able Team commandos gave any indication they were interested in Isaac or the men closing in on him. They walked straight ahead, looking past the group.

The kidnappers were perplexed. If these were the American specialists, why weren't they coming to Isaac's rescue? They glanced at Toni Blancanales, who they'd seen wave to Isaac. She'd spoken to both men, but neither had answered. They acted as if they hadn't heard her.

The terrorists' hesitation was the break Able Team needed. They split as if they were going to walk around the group, then at the last moment wheeled in, placing their bodies between the men holding the Quartermaster chairman and four other terrorists.

Lyons's hand shot between the captor and the captive, grabbing the hand that was likely holding a gun to Isaac's back. He yanked quickly, bringing the right hand out over the left arm, which was still gripping Isaac's wrist. The action was so sudden and quick that by the time the gunman squeezed the trigger the gun was no longer pointing at the hostage.

The bulky, square Webley Mark 1 barked once, sending a bullet straight into Lyons's midsection.

Pol stepped past his target, holding his *jo* high and by the middle, as if not wanting to trip someone with it. When he was within a few feet of his target, the *jo* blurred and the slight knob that formed the handle of the walking stick smashed into the kidnapper's temple. The man folded without a sound.

The *jo* swung back, and its tip dug into the solar plexus of the terrorist closest to Politician's back. The goon doubled over, struggling to breathe. The last two stepped back instead of trying to jump the Able Team warrior.

The eyes of the terrorist who had fired his gun bugged out. His victim's hold tightened to bone-crushing intensity instead of slacking.

Lyons's lips stretched in a tight, controlled grin as his right hand flashed up and two protruding knuckles smashed into the bulging eyes. The killer screamed in agony and dropped his Webley in a struggle to get away from the man he now saw as the devil.

Lyons shot his right hand back and then punched to his right, hoping to connect with the neck of the next goon. But the man danced out of reach.

"Allah is to thank!" he bellowed.

Instead of closing in, the kidnappers were fanning out around Isaac, Lyons, Blancanales and their two colleagues who were already victims of the Able Team counteroffensive.

One of the reluctant outer circle shouted to Isaac, "You come. We got your chauffeur." The voice had a harsh Slavic accent.

"Nice try, gentlemen," Isaac told Lyons and Politician, "but it looks as if they have the whip hand."

Lyons wasn't listening; he was exchanging glances with Gadgets. Gadgets gave an umpire's safe signal by spreading his arms. Lyons jerked his head almost imperceptibly. Once again Gadgets and Lao faded into the crowd.

Then Lyons gave the wrist he still had hold of a final twist, and the man dropped to the concrete floor.

Isaac pulled himself erect and took a step toward the kidnappers. Lyons held out his left arm to stop him and indicated the fallen terrorists with a sweep of his right hand.

"We'll trade your comrades here for the chauffeur."

"Infidel! They are ready to go to Allah for the cause."

"They won't be going to Allah. They'll be going to prison where scum like you deserve to rot."

One terrorist took a step toward Lyons, but his companion held him back.

The crowd had drawn well back at the sound of the gunshot. Airport security police were closing in from all directions. The terrorists immediately produced Webleys or sawed-off Lanchester subguns.

The ringleader ignored Lyons's threats and spoke again to Isaac. "You with the Zionist name. Explain to these imperialists that your chauffeur dies if they don't stay away."

Isaac looked up at Lyons, who nodded.

"Stay back," Isaac shouted at the security force. "These men are holding my chauffeur hostage."

One man in uniform stopped where he was and started talking into a compact radio communicator. The rest of the force stopped closing in and instead concentrated on moving the crowd back.

The terrorist Lyons had clipped wrenched his hand free. He alternated between rubbing his agonizing eyes and trying to stare at the powder burn on Lyons's shirt front. As he bent to pick up his automatic Lyons kneed him in the groin, sending him stumbling across the floor to fall at the feet of another terrorist.

GADGETS AND LAO HAD little information and almost no time in which to find and release the chauffeur. They had no idea where the car was parked.

Gadgets strode through the crowds, Lao at his heels, scanning the crowd. He finally spotted what he was looking for, a boy of twelve or thirteen who wasn't at the airport to do any traveling. The kid was looking to his right and then his left, trying to spot some luggage that wasn't sufficiently attended.

Gadgets strode past, then whirled and seized the boy.

"Cor! You got no right. I ain't done nuthin'."

Gadgets produced an American twenty, squatted so his head would be level with the boy's and handed him the bill. The boy examined the money carefully.

Satisfied that the business relationship was genuine, the boy asked, "Wot you want? I ain't got a sister, Yank."

"I want speed. The nobs with chauffeurs. Where would the cars wait?"

The kid nodded once and took off darting through the crowd as only a boy can. Gadgets and Lao were hardpressed to keep him in sight. It took constant use of sharp elbows, leaving a wake of indignation and curses.

The boy stopped by a set of doors and pointed at a no parking zone with three chauffeur-driven cars idling at the curb. One car, a gray Bentley, had two other men sitting in it, one in the front and one in the back.

Gadgets patted the boy once on the shoulder to indicate a job well done, then shoved him to one side. The Able Team commando and Lao Ti strode through the doors.

"Taxi!" Gadgets shouted, putting a lot of nasal into the *a* to exaggerate his American accent.

He yanked open the front door of the occupied Bentley while Lao opened the door to the rear of the car.

"Iss private!" the man in the back seat shouted in a heavy accent.

Lao paid no attention and climbed in. Her tiny build hardly made her seem any kind of threat. The occupant tried to straight-arm her back out of the car. His wrist was seized in a tight grip, and he was jerked in the direction of the open door. Before he realized he was under attack, he was stretched across the small woman's lap like a bad boy about to be spanked.

The spanking hand came down as a small fist, crashing into the lowest vertebra. The inferior cervical ganglion was traumatized, sending the whole system into shock. The hood was unconscious before he could figure out what was taking place.

Gadgets's target was less inclined to believe in the harmlessness of human beings—a group he had never really understood. When the front door began to open, he raised his Webley.

He never got a chance to fire it. As Gadgets opened the door, he turned as if he were going to slide into the front seat. Then his foot flashed out in a pile-driving side kick that smashed the gun hand into the gunman's chest before he could bring the weapon to bear.

Gadgets slid into the seat and grabbed the gunman's right hand in both of his. He bent the guy's wrist until the man howled with pain and dropped his weapon. Gadgets let go with his right hand and smashed his elbow back into the terrorist's windpipe. The man turned white and began to gag.

The Stony Man warrior stepped out of the car again, dragging his target by the hair. When he was clear of the car, a quick ax-hand chop rendered the gunman unconscious. Gadgets let him drop on the sidewalk. Lao dragged the other man out of the car and joined him.

When the chauffeur was sure the two men had been subdued he got out of the Bentley. "You must be some of the American specialists the guv'nor is supposed to be meeting,'' the chauffeur guessed. ''I think he's got the genuine kipper this time.''

''Hurry. We have to let Isaac know you're okay,'' Gadgets answered.

''I'm not going to argue with you folks,'' the chauffeur assured them.

Gadgets and Lao pocketed the awkward Webleys and set a furious pace back through the airport. The crowd around the standoff had grown, and it took all of Gadgets's and Lao's determination to force their way through quickly.

''THE PRICE HAS just gone up,'' the terrorist leader said, his voice quivering with anger. ''We will also take with us the barbarian who kicks our men as if they were dogs.''

''I don't kick dogs,'' Lyons replied. ''They're worthy of some respect.''

As he spoke, he was looking over the heads of the crowd, paying little attention to the Shiite terrorist.

''You'll not be so loose with your tongue when we're finished with you,'' the leader promised. ''The police have the crowd under control. It's time to start moving.''

Above the heads of the crowd, Gadgets's hand appeared, giving the ''V for Victory'' sign. Lyons let out his breath. He hadn't been sure if he could stall any longer.

''Okay. Let's go,'' Lyons said.

Suiting actions to words, he and Pol started walking toward the exit.

''Not yet!'' the terrorist leader shouted. ''We must make sure the imperialists understand what is to be done.''

But what was to be done was obvious. Pol and Lyons both leaped at the same time.

The first casualty was the group leader. He had moved inside the circle for protection from police snipers. Lyons's left hand darted out and pushed the leader's short Lanchester toward the ceiling two stories above. The Ironman's right fist introduced itself to the man's larynx.

The leader's protests became a garble of choking sounds. His knees buckled, and he sagged to the concrete floor with both hands clutching his throat, trying to convince it to pass something other than blood into his lungs.

Lyons's boot flashed out in a kick that would have made a National Football League player envious. The boot connected just under the terrorist's chin, lifting him clear of the floor to collapse like a broken toy.

Pol's *jo* swung in a short arc and broke the closest gun hand. He moved right past the terrorist who'd dropped his gun and lunged toward his next target like a fencer. The tip of the *jo* caught the man in the solar plexus, killing him instantly.

Then Politician straightened and swept the stick back, smashing the knee of the terrorist with the broken hand.

One of the two terrorists who had originally grabbed Isaac was still unconscious. At the first sign of battle, the other made a headfirst dive and retrieved his automatic.

Yelling "Infidel pig," he rolled onto one shoulder and shot Politician in the back.

Then he watched in frozen horror, unable to pull the trigger again. The Able Team warrior turned and stomped him with his heel, driving pieces of fractured rib into the gunman's lung.

A sudden hush fell over the vast terminal. The action was over, and dead terrorists littered the floor.

"What about my chauffeur?" Isaac asked. His voice reflected fear for the man's safety.

Just then Gadgets and Lao managed to push their way up to the police barricade with the chauffeur in tow.

"I'm right here, guv. These two saved me." The chauffeur looked around, but there was no sign of his two benefactors.

Then the London police arrived and took over. Lyons, Politician, Toni and Babette were escorted into special interview rooms where they were kept incommunicado until a Scotland Yard inspector arrived to do the interrogations.

DETECTIVE INSPECTOR OWEN QUINN was a massive man with thick black hair and a square chin that always seemed to need a shave. He'd been dispatched from Scotland Yard at the same time the SAS had sent a squad in response to the terrorism signal from airport security. The SAS call had been canceled before the group reached Heathrow, but the inspector still had a job to do, and he resented it.

He took his time and did a thorough interview with each detainee. The results only added to his frustration. Airport security had correctly separated the attackers from the victims and had given a concise report of as much action as they had seen. But Quinn wanted to know why this particular group was a terrorist target.

He started with the Muslims, without success. Each one glared at him and said nothing. One had been knocked out early in the action; there was some worry about concussion. The Scotland Yard detective was sure they weren't from the Middle East. They seemed East European to him.

The next had been booted unconscious while standing. Quinn had heard of these martial arts techniques, but he'd never heard of a high kick being used so effectively before. The terrorist had a badly fractured jaw. It was doubtful he could talk even if he'd wanted to.

The final survivor had a broken hand and a broken knee. The airport police had reported that a ''white-haired gentleman'' had taken his cane to the man.

In the end, all Quinn could do was have the men taken and booked by the uniformed branch. It was a frustrated detective inspector who turned his attention to the victims.

Whom should he tackle first? There were four Americans and two Britons, an influential-looking man and his chauffeur. He decided that self-preservation and the need for information dictated that he should start with the English gentleman.

Once he had the man's name, Isaac, and his occupation, Quinn thought he'd struck pay dirt.

''Now then, sir, can you tell me what this is all about?''

The short bald industrialist stared across the small scarred desk at the detective and thought of his employees.

Isaac knew he was in a bind. First, he didn't know for sure whether the attempt on him at the airport was connected with the extortion attempt that had prompted him to call in Able Group. None of the terrorists had said anything to make the connection.

The connection didn't matter. The promise to kill the employees of Quartermaster Software one at a time was the most terrifying threat anyone could make to Uriel Isaac. He considered each employee a member of his family. Each was mentioned in his will. His shares and his company went to them.

"I suppose it was some sort of kidnap attempt. They said nothing except that they were taking me with them. They threatened to kill my chauffeur if I didn't cooperate."

"They gave no indication as to what they intended?"

"None." So far, Isaac knew he'd told the detective nothing the man didn't already know.

"And who were the two gentlemen who took care of these men who tried to kidnap you?"

"I don't know."

"You don't know?" Quinn's voice was heavy with incredulity.

"Miss Blancanales might know. They seemed to have arrived on the same flight she did."

"You were here to meet Miss Blanca— What did you say that name was?"

Isaac spelled and pronounced the name for Quinn. Quinn repeated it until he had the pronunciation down smoothly.

"Now, who did you say she was?"

"I didn't, but she's the CEO of Able Group, an American security firm."

"And she was coming here to see you?" Quinn's frustration was beginning to show in his voice, although his words never lost their outward semblance of patience.

"Yes, her firm handles our security. Security is an important thing to any company connected with computers."

"So I understand, sir. What was this meeting about?"

"I'm not sure this has any connection to being attacked."

"Just answer the question, sir. We'll try to connect things later."

"No. Why am I being detained and cross-examined like a suspect when I was the object of the crime? You're treating me like a criminal."

"I shouldn't say that, sir."

"In that case, I'll be leaving."

It would have given Quinn great satisfaction to use his size twelve oxford to help the little man on his way. Instead, he had to swallow his anger and continue in a mild voice.

"We need a statement, sir."

"You've got it. I have no idea what this is about."

"Would you be so kind as to wait until I've had a chance to talk to the others? I'll try not to keep you too long."

Quinn was too smooth. Isaac knew he couldn't stave off an investigation.

"Very well," he finally conceded.

Quinn telephoned the Yard for help before moving on to question the chauffeur.

The chauffeur's story only added confusion to an already jumbled situation. The only people the chauffeur could describe didn't seem to be connected to this attempted kidnapping. Of course, by the time they got his story there was no sign of the two gunmen he claimed had gotten into his car. It would be hours before Quinn could get the detectives to start searching for verification of the chauffeur's story.

Seething with pent-up hostility, Quinn decided to see if the women would be easier picking.

The tall one was hopeless. She simply kept repeating that she wanted a lawyer. Quinn stomped out in disgust and strode into the waiting room where they were holding the smaller woman. Quinn had to admit she was easy to look at and definitely had class, for an American. She opened the conversation.

"You look frustrated, Inspector."

"I am. No one wants to admit he knows what this whole mess is about. I have dead men to account for and no indication what this is all about."

"I don't think anyone knows. I saw it all and not once did the gunmen say what they wanted."

"What can you tell me? Why are you here?"

"I'm here on business for a client, Quartermaster Software. I'm not free to tell you that business if Mr. Isaac hasn't. I would if I had any indication that our business is relevant. I have no such indication."

Quinn rubbed a hand over his jaw. The rasp of calluses over stubble sounded loud in the small room. The call from the Yard had sent him out of his house without time for a shave or a cup of tea. He brought his mind back to the problem of getting this woman to talk.

"What is your position with Able Group, Miss Blancanales?

"President and general manager."

"And the other members of your group are employees?"

She shook her head. "Rosario Blancanales is my brother. He and Hermann Schwarz are the senior partners of the firm. However, the day-to-day operation is left up to me."

"That leaves the tall blond gentleman and the two other women."

"The tall blond *gentleman* and the short Oriental are associates of Rosario and Hermann. The very tall woman is a gymnast and a friend of Hermann's."

Quinn detected the accent on the word "gentleman" and picked up the trail like a hound.

"You don't seem particularly fond of the blond American."

"Carl's all right. It's just that he's the chief of another operation, and I hate to see Rosario and Hermann defer to him out of habit. Lyons doesn't know a thing about business and has all the tact of a bull elephant on the rampage."

"That's a strange way of putting it. What's this 'other operation'?"

"You'll have to talk to them about that."

She was too cool. Quinn knew he'd have a better chance breaking the professional terrorists than he would the female American executive. Still, he wasn't angry at her. She had too much class.

The white-haired American with the deadly cane was much more helpful. He identified himself as a senior partner in Able Group, the brother of Miss Blancanales.

"Miss Blancanales mentioned that you work with a Mr. Lyons in some other way. She was vague. Would you please elaborate?" Quinn asked.

Blancanales shook his head. "Nothing to do with this."

Quinn was puzzled. Were these four involved in some sort of criminal activity? He made a mental note to ask the FBI for cooperation and then decided to try a change of topic.

"Why are you in the United Kingdom?"

"I had the time and have never met the officers of Quartermaster Software. So I thought I'd come along and meet them."

"Then they didn't expect you?"

"Not unless Toni told them I was coming."

Quinn decided to change his approach once again. "That's a deadly stick you carry."

"Sticks aren't deadly."

"Not deadly! There are several corpses out there who would beg to differ. It could be classified as a concealed weapon."

"It wasn't concealed and it's not a weapon."

"Do you require a walking stick to get around, sir?"

Politician grinned his most disarming grin. "I hope not. But I certainly require one to stay alive in a London airport."

"Come, come, sir. There's more to it than that. One of the airport chaps claims you were shot in the back."

"I was. My bulletproof underwear must have stopped it."

"Your what?"

Silently Politician pulled off his jacket and shirt.

"Damn me," said Quinn, "if it isn't a flak jacket done up as skivvies. Why do you wear that, sir?"

"I always like to be prepared for the unexpected."

"The United Kingdom is not a battle zone," Quinn rumbled defensively.

Politician merely raised an eyebrow.

Quinn was stung. "I'll have to take that stick, sir."

"I'll need a lawyer to advise me on that. I'll hang on to it until I get a lawyer."

"It's evidence."

"Evidence? Am I being accused of doing something?"

"You killed men with that today."

"I admit it. Should I have just stood there instead?"

"I'll have to insist." The pulse in Quinn's forehead throbbed.

"I'll keep it here until I've had benefit of legal counsel."

Quinn stomped out of the room and stormed into the employee lounge where airport security were holding the other American.

Quinn stopped in his tracks when the first thing the large blond man said was, "Long live the republic."

"What republic?" Quinn demanded. "Are you Irish?"

"American. Any damn republic. Down with monarchies. They try to kill you the moment you land."

"Come, come now, Mr. Lyons. Let's get right to the point. What is your occupation?"

"Human target. Walking corpse. Victim of the monarchy."

"You seem very much alive, which is more than I can say for the chaps you went up against."

Lyons indicated his powder-burned shirt. "They tried. I notice that you didn't show until the battle was over."

"Surely you're not suggesting I had something to do with the attack on your party?"

"We weren't having a party. Why am I a prisoner while men who fire guns in crowded public buildings are allowed to roam the street?"

Quinn sighed. "I suppose you want a lawyer, too."

"Why should I want a lawyer? Will he buy me a new shirt? I want a reporter. I want the world to know what you do to Americans."

Quinn looked into the blue eyes. They sparkled with madness and cold calculation. Quinn did the only thing he could figure to do. He beat a hasty retreat.

By that time the reinforcements had arrived. He decided to put two units of three detectives each on the tail of the two American men when they were released. He'd have a difficult time explaining that move to the commander, but he trusted his nose. Those two Americans may have been victims, but they were also a hell of a lot more than wacky businessmen.

Quinn's only moment of triumph came when Isaac's solicitor told Blancanales that the police had a right to take the cane, at least until after the inquest.

He watched the four men and two women disappear into the crowd at the airport. The inspector was sure he was going to have a better opportunity to grill them in the future. There was a lot more to that party than met the eye.

He turned his head and glanced idly at a redheaded photographer who followed the group out of the building. It would have been nice if someone had photographs of what really had gone on. He shrugged away his wishful thinking and went to find his car.

3

"Give terrorists what they want and you breed more terrorists," Lyons growled. "It's short-term gain for long-term pain."

Everyone else around the boardroom table exchanged agonized glances. Nate Zimmerman, Uriel Isaac and four employee/shareholders elected by the other employees formed the board of directors of Quartermaster Software. They were dressed informally by British boardroom standards but their conservative suits were very formal in comparison to those worn in American companies.

Toni fitted in easily. Politician and Gadgets looked like poor cousins in suits meant for the tropics. Lao Ti had exchanged her usual jeans and work shirt for a full skirt and Chinese jacket. Lyons stood out like a weed in a flower garden in his checked sport jacket and yellow shirt with the powder burn dead center.

Babette had decided not to attend the meeting. She'd taken the time to go shopping for clothes more suited to London's chilly November.

Quartermaster Software was located in the Chelsea district of London. Once a bohemian and literary enclave, Chelsea was now home to professional offices and boutiques. Quartermaster had taken over a four-story Georgian house, a square building with time-blackened bricks and flashing white trim. It looked more like a small apartment building to North American eyes.

The boardroom was located on the top floor, furnished with a thirty-foot-long Queen Anne table and uncomfortable straight-backed chairs. Two ornate chandeliers, each glittering with hundreds of pounds of crystal, lit the table. The only thing in the room that wasn't ramrod straight was Ironman's yellow shirt. He slouched on his tailbone while everybody else sat up as if they were on inspection.

Isaac had opened the meeting by giving a full report of everything that had happened to date. Then a board member had suggested it would be cheaper to pay off the terrorists and get back to work. That had prompted Lyons's unwanted observation.

Toni opened her mouth to make an angry reply, but Politician put a hand over hers and hastened to speak first.

"It's usually more cost-effective to make the payoff and then hunt for the extortionists."

"This isn't usual," Lyons muttered.

Toni smoothly moved in to reestablish control of Able Group's relationship with their client.

"That may be so, Carl, however—"

"Hold it, Toni," Gadgets snapped. He received a glare from the small dark-haired woman but ignored it to ask Lyons, "What's unusual?"

Ironman simply stared at Gadgets without saying a thing.

"Hey, this is your old friend Hermann Schwarz. Remember? What's unusual about this situation?"

Since the Able Team commandos weren't on Stony Man business, they were traveling on their own passports. Ironman had simply been introduced as Carl Lyons. Since no title had been given, the executive and directors of Quartermaster assumed he was an employee of Able Group. They now sat in confused silence as a partner of the firm begged Lyons for information.

"We're not following our standing operating procedures."

Politician and Gadgets exchanged blank looks, oblivious to the stares of everyone else around the table.

Gadgets snapped his fingers and muttered, "Oh, shit!" He turned to Isaac and said, "We'd like a ten-minute break before this goes any farther."

Isaac nodded, unable to hide his disappointment that Able Group hadn't been able to put its act together before the meeting began. He seemed to expect a partner to take the big blond guy out and read the riot act to him. That didn't happen.

Instead, Gadgets asked, "Will you have someone bring up my bag, please?"

Isaac did so, then the eleven people sat in strained silence. The six members of Quartermaster were at one end of the long table, Able Team, Lao Ti and Toni at the other.

The Quartermaster contingent stared at Lyons in puzzlement. Toni stared at all three Stony Man warriors, barely able to contain her anger. Only Lao Ti sat back, relaxed, apparently indifferent to the whole affair.

"I don't see—" Toni began.

"Just wait," Pol interrupted.

After that everyone sat in edgy silence until there was a timid knock at the door and Isaac's chauffeur appeared, carrying Gadgets's large piece of luggage.

Gadgets took it from the man and rummaged around until he produced a gray metal box. He flicked switches and began to sweep the room.

"There's no need for that," one Quartermaster board member said. "Our own security sweeps the entire premises once a week."

He had to raise his voice to finish the sentence when Gadgets's gray box suddenly began to howl louder as he approached the telephone on the boardroom table.

Gadgets turned off his sweeper and tackled the handset on the telephone. He took out the transmitter button and then swept the set again. No sound. He swept the room once more, but it was clean.

As Gadgets was finishing his second sweep, Politician turned to the Quartermaster board member who had just spoken. "Have security bring up the detector they use."

"Do you mean right now?" Isaac asked.

"I mean right now."

Gadgets packed up his sweeper, threw his bag into a corner and sat down again. Since the telephone was no longer functional, the board member was forced to leave the room and go to security in person. Once again there was a tense silence as they waited for the director-turned-messenger to return.

The bug sweeper, when it was delivered, was four times the size of the one Gadgets used, and it seemed more elaborate, with several dials and a row of buttons and adjustments. Gadgets accepted it silently, put it on the table and, producing a screwdriver from his jacket pocket, opened it up.

As he worked, Gadgets asked, "Who's the bloker joker who did the switcheroo?"

"I beg your pardon?" said the board member who had delivered the sweeper.

"This isn't the sweeper Able Group provided."

"No," another director admitted. "The one your company supplied took too long to warm up. When we were offered newer technology at a decent price, we jumped at the chance. This one works the instant it's turned on."

"Great," Gadgets muttered. "But that means it doesn't have a self-test feature."

"I beg your pardon?"

"You should, brother. Able Group supplies sweepers that test all their own circuits before you can start to sweep."

While he spoke, Gadgets poked and prodded the wiring and printed circuit plates until he found a wire wrapped in electrician's tape.

He peeled off the tape and said, "Fasten your eyes on your super-duper 'new' technology."

Some of the directors left their chairs to peer at Gadgets's exhibit. When the tape was removed, it was obvious that the wire had been cut with snips and not rejoined. The tape concealed the fact that the wire had been cut and no longer conducted current.

Politician turned to Lyons. "Now, will you tell us what's unusual about this situation?"

Lyons shrugged. "They know this place inside out. They know Isaac has an emergency buzzer, and when he presses it. They knew we were being met at Heathrow. Either it's insiders or the place is wired tighter than a radio studio, or both."

"Why didn't you just say that you thought the room might be bugged?" Toni demanded.

"No point," Lyons replied.

Politician explained his partner's reaction to his sister and the members of the Quartermaster board of directors. "Ironman doesn't like sloppy work. It was our job to check the room before the meeting began, but we assumed your security department had things in hand. We should have known better. Now, let's get down to a planning session."

If the ambiguous relationship between Carl Lyons and the owners of Able Group was a mystery to the directors of Quartermaster, planning sessions were not.

"What are the objectives?" one of them asked.

There was a moment's silence as people struggled to define what was needed to preserve the lives of everyone connected with Quartermaster. Lyons didn't have the patience to wait for the amateurs to give their opinion. Able Team fought terrorists constantly. He knew exactly what had to be done.

"The terrorists must be eliminated," he rumbled at the group.

"We'd be happy if we could see them jailed," Isaac answered. "But that part of it's up to the police."

"The police haven't been threatened," Lyons said.

Politician turned to Lyons. "Let me handle this."

The icy warrior gave a minute nod and leaned back.

Politician fidgeted with the pad and pencil that had been placed in front of him on the table. The rest waited impatiently for him to get his thoughts in order.

"Mr. Lyons is right," Pol told them. "However, this is a case where the correct answer may not be the acceptable answer."

He paused, but saw that the puzzled expressions on the directors' faces remained, so he had to pick up the ball again. "This isn't simply a case of paying a ransom for an executive. The terrorists have physically penetrated your building. They've listened to you work. Now they're demanding protection money. The demand appears to be a one-time thing, but there's no reason they won't hit you again and again until you're bled dry. They aren't going to tell you what their intention is. If they make it seem like a one-time demand, you're less apt to fight. But you can be sure that as long as they can get money and technology in exchange for mere threats, they'll keep coming back."

The Quartermaster directors stared at one another in horror. They hadn't considered the long-term implications.

"And exactly what are you suggesting?" Isaac demanded.

"LID," Lyons muttered.

Gadgets laughed. "Wild, baby. They'll flip."

Toni was watching the proceedings and frowning. She knew her business and recognized the problem. Giving in to the threats would mean that Quartermaster Software would be bled to death. Taking positive action to eliminate the terrorists would lead to reprisals—employees' deaths. It was a no-win situation. She damned Ironman for pointing it out, even though she knew he was right. It boiled down to a problem Able Group couldn't solve. Quartermaster Software was dead and maybe some of its employees as well.

Politician found himself once again shouldering the unpleasant task of explaining the facts of life to the directors.

"LID, in some form, is the only hope we've got. No business has ever attempted it before. The Israeli government has been the only democratically elected government with the guts to use those tactics. It doesn't make the country popular, even with other victims of terrorism."

"What is it?" someone asked.

"An acronym for the only way known to stop terrorists. Locate. Identify. Destroy."

"I say, are you suggesting we hire you to kill whoever's threatening us?" Isaac demanded.

"We'll simply put guards on the premises," another director stated.

Politician answered the second comment first. "And will you put guards in the home of each employee and assign other guards to follow them to the supermarket and the theater?"

"That's what we have police for."

"And if the terrorists don't strike for two weeks, will the police maintain full bodyguard protection on everyone who works here? And on your customers?"

"Our customers?" The voice expressed shock.

"Of course. If they're determined, they'll hit you somehow. And you know the police haven't the manpower to protect your entire staff."

"And you suggest we hire you to kill the terrorists first?"

Pol shook his head. "We're not hired killers. We'll shoot to kill when necessary. That's not the same thing. But the gang must be broken up and each member accounted for. Whether he's killed, is sent to jail or is simply chased from the country in such a way that he doesn't dare return, doesn't matter. The essential thing is that the gang be destroyed."

"Don't you think it would be cheaper just to give these terrorist chaps what they want?" a director demanded.

Lyons turned his cold eyes on the man.

"Do you?" Lyons demanded.

"It's difficult to know."

"How many times do you wish to pay off to be sure?" Lyons pressed.

"Just once."

"We agree."

"I don't understand."

Pol sighed. He knew Lyons wouldn't bother explaining.

"You have no choice. You have to pay them this time. There's no other way to keep your employees alive. But, if you don't use this payment to locate and identify your enemy, you'll have to pay off the next time as well."

"I'm not sure I follow your reasoning," Isaac said.

"The payoff is our only link with the terrorists. They don't play games. Look what happened to the president of Gammabase Delta and the so-called expert they employed."

Two of the directors shuddered. Van Nice had been blown to bits. Edwards had been hacked into small pieces and dumped into a canal. The high-tech industries formed a tight-knit community where everyone knew everyone else. The glances the directors exchanged indicated the respect they'd had for Edwards. Politician had made his point.

Pol continued, "If you don't use this payoff to identify your enemy, you'll be in exactly the same position you're in now the next time someone phones to demand both cash and technology."

The five directors of Quartermaster looked at one another, holding a silent debate.

"What happens if and when you succeed in identifying these extortionists?" Zimmerman asked.

Pol hurried to answer before Lyons could. "We can't cross that bridge until we come to it. Hopefully, we can get enough information to allow Scotland Yard to take over."

"We could call Scotland Yard now."

"Why don't you? Why didn't you before this?" Gadgets demanded.

"We knew we were being watched. We were afraid they'd kill several of our people in retaliation," Zimmerman admitted.

"In other words, you already knew the enemy had to be eliminated," Lyons snapped.

ON THE OTHER SIDE of the same block, another strategy meeting was taking place. Aya Jishin sat at the scarred metal desk. The turned-up corner had been pounded down, leaving jagged metal along the underside.

Yoru's squat form occupied the only other chair in the room. Four other men and one woman stood around the room, giving each one an unrestricted line of sight to Jishin and her lieutenant. The air was already stale in the minuscule, dingy office.

"The bug in the boardroom telephone went dead a little while ago," Jishin informed the group. "We expect the other devices to be found soon."

"It's surprising that they haven't disconnected them by now," Yoru interrupted. His voice contrasted sharply to Jishin's. It was smooth and held traces of a British accent.

Jishin glared at her lieutenant, then picked up the thread of her briefing once again.

"You must increase the pressure and not give them time to organize. According to the photographer, the Americans neutralized an eight-member team sent to snatch Uriel Isaac. I don't understand how eight armed men were killed or captured by six unarmed Americans. But those who survived will pay the price of incompetence."

Two of the men standing along the wall shuddered. They didn't need to be told the fate waiting those Jishin declared incompetent. Others had failed, but only once.

Jishin stared at them, then she continued, "I am not going to be here to direct this campaign, but it must go as smoothly as if I directed it myself. Because I must be in the United States to set up our main operation, Yoru will be in charge. When you have the money and the technology, you are to join me in Danvers. Push up delivery to four o'clock Monday. Have everything ready. The first thing to check—''

She was interrupted by a knock on the door. Jishin nodded, and the terrorist standing nearest the door opened it. The photographer barged into the crowded room with a fistful of eight-by-ten glossy prints.

He was a tall man, six foot three, and very thin. He had a beaked nose and eyes a color that shifted between blue and green. When he spoke, his voice was high, like a boy's.

''I had the lab rush through the prints, just as you told me.''

He dumped the glossies on Jishin's desk and would have made a quick exit if she hadn't stopped him.

''Stay,'' she barked, as if she were training a dog.

He turned and looked at her nervously.

''I may have questions.''

With everyone in the room watching her, she began to flip through the photographs, which were grainy but sharp. Her hand paused at the third one, and her pasty complexion faded two shades lighter. She looked at the next and slammed it on the desk before she scanned the last three prints.

The photographer began to quiver and backed up until he could steady himself with one hand on the door. Jishin looked up and pinned him with her beady eyes.

''Good shots. Now fuck off.''

The photographer's hand slipped off the doorknob twice before he yanked the door open and ran into the hall.

''It's them,'' Jishin barked. ''It's those accursed pigs.''

Yoru was the only one with enough nerve to ask, ''Who?''

Jishin glared at him. The silence stretched until people were holding their breath. When Jishin finally spoke, they let their breath out slowly.

"This project was started once before, under other sponsorship. It failed, causing me great loss of face. It failed because of the six people who arrived on the plane today."

Jishin paused and thought for a moment before continuing. "I must be in America tomorrow. The plan is the more important thing. It is up to you to see that those six are eliminated. Take no chances. They are dangerous.

"Kill them before you go ahead with Quartermaster Software. It is the only way you will succeed. And you all know the cost of failure. In this case, it will be a slow death. They must not be allowed to live!"

Everyone nodded.

"Good. We have just enough time before I leave for my plane. Let's plan carefully."

4

"I managed to arrange additional rooms at your hotel," Isaac told Toni Blancanales. His face conveyed the apology that he kept out of his voice.

Toni nodded her understanding. The terrorists knew where she and Able Team were staying. They'd have to change quarters. Toni's mind searched for a safe topic of conversation.

"My associates came straight here from a vacation in Hawaii," she told Isaac. "We're going to have to find them more appropriate clothing very quickly. What do you suggest?"

Isaac thought for a moment. "Let me ask my tailor." He pulled over the telephone, dialed and explained the situation to someone he called Joc. Then he listened for a minute before saying, "Let me check on that. Hold on."

Isaac covered the mouthpiece and told Toni, "My tailor says that if you'll get the men to his shop right after lunch, he'll measure them. Then he'll buy off the rack at a quality store and make any alterations required. The suits won't be perfect, but they'll be ready by tomorrow afternoon."

"That would be terrific!"

Isaac returned to the telephone. "That's acceptable. Expect them after lunch. Right."

Isaac gave Toni the address in Shepherd Market and described how to get there from the Intercontinental Hotel where he'd booked Toni and Able Team.

The talk then drifted to their golf scores until there was a tap on the door and Gadgets stuck his head inside.

"Babette's back from shopping. We can go anytime you're ready."

Toni stood up. "We were waiting for you. Through here?"

Gadgets nodded.

Toni shook hands with Isaac, who said, "Abner's waiting to drive you back to the hotel."

The trip along King's Road and north on Grosvenor to Hyde Park Corner took less than ten minutes. Toni started to ask Gadgets what he'd found, but the electronics whiz shook his head and kept the conversation on Babette's shopping.

Babette had exchanged her light linen suit for wool pants and a sweater. She wore comfortable running shoes—even if their color clashed with her outfit. The shoes were hot pink.

LYONS TRIED TO PACE around the room, but the telephone cord pulled him up short. For a moment, Politician was worried Ironman might decide to yank the cord out of the wall.

"I'm telling you now," Lyons roared into the mouthpiece, "we're on legitimate antiterrorist business, and yes, American interests are at stake. We need weapons, and we need someone who knows the ropes."

Pol sat still, listening. Aaron Kurtzman's voice came across the Atlantic from Stony Man distinctly and loudly enough that Pol could just catch the words.

"Helping Gadgets and Pol run their company isn't a Stony Man op," the assignments officer insisted. "We couldn't explain to the British government why we're supplying you with weapons. Forget it."

"Shit. Let me talk to Brognola."

"He's in transit, on the way to Milan for an antiterrorist conference," yelled Kurtzman, who was affectionately known as "the Bear" around Stony Man Farm.

"These industries are being hit hard for both money and technology. How much British technology do you want to dump into the Reds' hands?"

"Don't be insulting. You're on foreign soil on private business. We don't dare help you."

Lyons kicked one of the twin beds, dumping the mattress onto the floor.

"Let me talk to David McCarter."

"Keep McCarter out of this."

"He's on his own time. Phoenix Force isn't on a mission. Put him on the damn phone."

"Your holiday is over. I want Able Team to report for duty in two days' time," Kurtzman barked.

Lyons frowned at the telephone, his bad temper evaporated. This wasn't Kurtzman. What the hell was happening?

Politician mouthed the words, "Bugged line."

Lyons thought about it. Able team had a scrambler, but it was still in Gadgets's bag. An insecure line could explain the Bear's insistence that they go by the book. In either case, there was only one way to play the hand.

"Can you hear me, or have you already smashed the telephone?" the voice asked.

"I hear you loud and clear. We all quit."

"Can you speak for the rest of them?"

Lyons thought for a moment before saying, "Yes. Damn it, yes."

"I'll have the severance arrangements made." Kurtzman's voice froze telephone lines all the way across the ocean.

"Just put McCarter on. He's off duty."

"I can't stop him from talking to you. But if I were you, I'd be careful, Mr. Lyons."

Kurtzman's stilted speech was the clincher. He was definitely talking for the benefit of some unknown listener.

McCarter's informal approach was a relief after the stilted struggle with the Bear.

"Well, mate? What's got your pecker in a sling this time?"

"You off duty?" Lyons asked.

"Until these clods decide once again that the world's going to end tomorrow. What do you have in mind?"

"If you're for hire, we could use a guide in jolly old England."

"What do guides make these days?" McCarter asked. He always needed money.

"Five thousand pounds for a week's vacation."

"I'll bet a tour guide gets a swell vacation," McCarter quipped. "I'll be in on the first flight tomorrow morning." He hung up before Lyons could say anything more, apparently also worried about the telephone lines.

Lyons replaced the telephone handset, but before he could speak someone rapped on the door. Three long strides moved him behind the door before it opened. Politician remained on the bed to attract the attention of whoever was coming through the door.

"Come in," he called.

The door swung open, but there was no one in the doorway.

"Come on in, Gadgets," Pol invited, relaxing.

Gadgets ushered the two women into the room and closed the door. He looked around and asked, "How did you know it wasn't Lao?"

"She'd have arrived alone. I heard people in the hall."

Toni realized her pumps had been the only shoes to make any sound in the carpeted hall. She suddenly felt awkward in comparison to Babette's gymnast-trained body and Lao's silent glide that came from a lifetime of daily martial arts training.

"You people always go in and out of rooms like you were doing a grade-B movie?" she snapped.

"We're usually careful," her brother conceded.

"Especially when we're unarmed and we expect a terrorist attack," Gadgets added.

"That reminds me—" Toni began, but Lyons cut her off.

"Let's go for a walk."

Toni tried twice more to start a conversation, but each time she was silenced with a glare. They took the elevator down to the ground floor. When they were in the lobby, Lyons led the way to a small grouping of chairs and sat down. Glaring angrily, Toni was the last to sit.

"You got a beef?" Lyons demanded.

Toni stared at him as she leaned back and crossed her legs below the knees.

"I must admit," she began, "that I'm somewhat puzzled by your actions. I really appreciate your coming along, although I think Rosario and Hermann could handle things very well."

"What's that mean in English?"

Toni made a gesture of exasperation.

Pol slid into the conversation. "It means she thinks you're taking over her op."

"The hell I am."

Toni managed a strained smile. "I had some information for you. Instead of listening, you demand we take a walk. I appreciate your ability, but this is an Able Group operation. I'd like Able Group to appear to know what it's doing."

"Then don't include me in your fuck-ups."

Toni fought to control her temper. "If you don't have the information, I don't understand why you think I've 'fucked up,' to use your phrase."

"The boardroom all over again," Lyons growled.

Toni turned to Pol. "I think we both need a translator."

Politician laughed. "Everyone needs a translator when they deal with Ironman. In this case, if you have a message for him, you have to assure him that the room is bug-free or that it doesn't matter if the message is overheard.

"Ironman figures Quartermaster booked our rooms."

"They did," Toni confirmed. "That was the first part of the message."

"So, it's conceivable the rooms are bugged. We've learned to be careful of what we say in bugged rooms," Pol said.

Toni nodded. She didn't like the way things were going, but they made sense in a ruthless way that made her shudder.

"What else do you have for us?" Gadgets asked.

"Suits. You all have appointments with Isaac's tailor after lunch. He's going to buy three suits off the rack and alter them to fit. You'll have something presentable by tomorrow afternoon."

The three men exchanged glances and nodded.

"Thanks," Pol told her. "We'll grab a bite when Lao shows up."

"Where did she go?"

"Back to the airport," Gadgets answered. "We ditched a couple of terrorist handguns there, in case we were searched. She's gone to pick them up."

"McCarter will be joining us tomorrow morning," Pol told Gadgets, who nodded.

"Someone else?" Toni asked, her voice too sweet.

Gadgets laughed. "Yeah. You're so bugged by Lyons they're bringing in someone who'll make Ironman look like a real gentleman."

Toni rolled her eyes but said nothing.

"Now, can we eat?" Lyons begged. He sounded so unlike himself that everyone laughed.

Gadgets stood up. "Stop being so humble, Ironman. You'll choke on it."

"Shouldn't we wait for Lao?" Toni asked.

"She's here," Politician told her.

Toni was shaken to find the small woman sitting away from the group, watching them. She had a crumpled paper bag in her hand. Toni didn't have to be told what it contained.

THE TRIP TO THE TAILOR'S SHOP in Shepherd Market wasn't the simple thing Toni had envisioned. First, there was a detour to the nearest bank where Politician and Gadgets insisted that Toni arrange a transfer of company funds to replenish Able Team's diminishing money supply. She was outvoted and forced to do so, although she believed they had adequate funds with them.

Then Politician stopped at several places until he found a new walking stick that suited him. He finally settled on a straight black stick with a gold-plated brass knob for a head and a small steel ferrule on the tip.

Shepherd Market turned out to be a small cobblestoned mews that was closed off to traffic. Fruit markets, restaurants and boutiques all spilled out into the street. The brick buildings ranged from three to five stories high, turning the market into a series of canyons. The brickwork showed a century or two of London grime, but the wooden trim was painted and well cared for.

Able Team paused before entering the mews. They seemed to be testing the air like foxes before going to their lair. Then they split up. Politician and Lyons walked close to the buildings on one side of the mews; Lao, Babette and Gadgets went single file, hugging the buildings on the other side. Toni angrily walked down the middle to express her annoyance at their paranoia.

The tailor's shop was above a grocer's, with only a small sign in the window to announce its presence. Lao went up first. The rest stood around the doorway, watching the street until they received the all-clear signal.

Fitting the three men turned out to be quite the procedure. They were bulky from the flak jackets under their shirts. The dour Scottish tailor had a frown of disapproval on his face. Toni couldn't guess whether it was habitual or a comment on the clients Isaac had sent him. Certainly the tailor could tell that the men were demanding room for underarm holsters.

However, when it came time to indicate an approximate choice of materials, the diversity was amazing. Politician wanted only gray. Gadgets indicated a preference for a light blue, which caused the tailor's assistant to raise an eyebrow. Lyons indicated he would accept anything bright. The assistant hurried to the back room.

When Able Team and Babette once again took to the stairs, Toni lingered to pay a deposit on the order. An extra fifty pounds changed hands before the tailor would assure her that he would be unable to find anything except conservative business suits. Toni could see that Joc was wondering whether the extra fifty pounds was worth crossing the three grim-faced men.

Toni hurried to catch up with the rest, only to find them waiting at the foot of the stairs, cautiously sizing up the people in the street. With an exclamation of annoyance, Toni pushed past the group and marched out into Shepherd Market. She managed three paces before a bullet slammed into her shoulder.

She staggered, but would have kept her balance if a force like a hurtling freight train hadn't bowled her onto the hard, flat paving stones and pinned her down. She didn't have breath to speak, but realized Lyons was covering her body with his own.

Gadgets leaped and rolled into the street, firing his confiscated Webley at the rooftop opposite him. The moment Gadgets was in motion, Lyons was on his feet. He picked Toni up with one arm under her knees and another around her back and sprinted for a doorway, carrying her as easily as if she were a young child.

Toni's eyes could barely see above his shoulder. Two men were on a roof across from the tailor's shop. They were firing single shots rapidly, using some form of assault rifle. She couldn't tell what kind of rifles they were from that distance. Toni was sure a couple of the bullets had hit Lyons in the back. Suddenly those flak jackets no longer seemed so ridiculous.

Lyons hit a door with his shoulder, splintering the latch. Then they were inside, away from the war zone that had once been the peaceful market. She could hear the screams and the panicked stampede of shoppers and stall vendors, running for safety. Then the doorway darkened as Politician ran through.

They moved toward another doorway that led them into a stairwell. There was no place to go but up. Ironman took the steps three at a time. Pol was right behind. At the top of the stairs, Politician knocked gently on the door of an apartment that occupied the rear part of the building. A demanding knock might not have brought a response with the sound of gunfire in the street, but the almost timid sound caused the woman inside to open her door.

"My sister's been hit by a bullet. Could we put her down someplace and call for an ambulance?" Politician asked. His voice was so gentle that the alarm faded from the elderly woman's face.

Without saying a word, she led them to a small spotless bedroom. Politician indicated that Lyons should place Toni on the mat instead of the bed. The woman was shocked.

"Put the poor wee thing on the bed," the old woman demanded. "She'll not die on my floor."

"She won't die. I have to stop the bleeding. Get me something I can tear into strips for bandages." This time Pol's voice was firm, authoritative.

When the woman reappeared with a clean sheet in her hands, Lyons moved to the back of the flat. He found himself in a small kitchen. The window opened onto a fire escape. He opened the window, climbed out, shut it, then moved upward.

GADGETS EXPENDED all seven rounds of the Webley in a hail of fire that kept the terrorists' heads down on the opposite roof. It had bought enough time for Lyons and Pol to get

Toni safely inside another building. But the angle from which he was firing had not allowed him to score any direct hits with the unfamiliar weapon. Schwarz quickly found himself alone in the middle of the street with an empty weapon in his hand.

He took a long dive and rolled among the boxes under a fruit stand to avoid another hail of bullets from the rooftop. He crawled carefully, trying not to give away his position as bullets slammed through fruit and the wooden slats of the stand to smash into the paving stones around him.

Gadgets worked his way cautiously toward the edge of the stand closest to the snipers. His best chance was to reach the wall directly under them. Shooting straight down would be difficult for the terrorists. As he dodged from one stand to another, a bullet came precariously close to nicking his shoulder. Gadgets hit the pavement.

The doorway to the snipers' building was only ten feet from where Gadgets lay. He looked right and then left.

Additional armed men and women were storming in each entrance to the market.

LAO AND BABETTE WERE STILL on the stairs to the tailor's shop when the three men burst out to rescue Toni. The two women turned and raced back into the building. They ran up to the top floor, then down the hall, but couldn't find any way to the roof.

Babette seized a fire extinguisher from a wall bracket and smashed out the lower pane of a window at the end of the hall. The window didn't overlook the market square.

She then grabbed the crossbar above the broken window, leaned out as far as her arms would allow and looked up toward the roof. Her next action was to bounce up and down, checking to see if the crossbar would hold her weight. Then she was back inside, peeling off her sweater. She was grateful that she'd changed into running shoes.

The gymnast smashed out the upper pane and carefully removed glass splinters from the crossbar. Then she backed down the hall and sprinted toward the window. At the last moment, she leaped, and feet first, jumped through the opening.

She caught the crossbar and converted her outward energy into an upward swing. Suddenly she was hanging upside down, with the top of her head just below the upper edge of the window. Babette had succeeded in hooking her feet over the top of the roof parapet. "Up," she ordered Lao.

Lao looked out the window. She didn't pause but scrambled up the length of Babette's body and onto the roof. She then squatted on the parapet, grabbed one of Babette's legs and slowly rose from her squat. When the knee was above the edge of the wall, Lao twisted Babette's leg, then bent the knee over the parapet. Babette's other leg shot up and hooked itself over the bricks. Lao clung to the two legs while the gymnast curled her body up and forward until she rolled onto the roof.

The two women crept to the front of the roof and cautiously peered over. Across Shepherd Market the two gunmen on the rooftop were firing down into a fruit stall.

Lao produced a Webley from an inside pocket of her jacket. From a kneeling position, she took a two-hand grip and carefully squeezed off a shot. Across the gap a gunman dropped his Sterling assault rifle and clutched his gut. He curled forward until he fell onto his face.

Alerted by the death of his partner, the other terrorist swept his rifle up to rake the opposite roof. Lao held her position and calmly lined up the Webley's sights on the second gunman. Bullets began eating the roof around her. She squeezed off two shots. The first hit a shoulder and caused the gunman to spin away from his line of fire. He tumbled sideways, and the next bullet sliced his neck, opening the carotid artery. Blood gushed onto the roof. The killer dropped his weapon and spent his final seconds with his hands wrapped around his throat, feeling his life flow out between his fingers.

"Go for the door," Lao called out to Gadgets. Then she turned the automatic on one armed group running into the market.

Gadgets came out from under the stand as if he'd been shot from a cannon. He charged through the doorway straight ahead of him. A few bullets followed him, coming from some spot off to his left. To his right, the terrorists were too busy trying to dodge Lao's bullets to worry about the Able Team warrior.

Lao's automatic slammed in empty. She threw herself behind the low brick parapet just as a stream of bullets sought her position. She found herself facing Babette, who had to content herself with staying out of the line of fire because she had no weapon. The two women listened to the sound of sirens coming from several directions.

LYONS REACHED THE ROOF of the building in time to see the two snipers drop out of contention and enemy infantry run into the market from every entrance. A quick glance around the roof showed a pile of repair materials left by a workman. There were two five-gallon containers of congealed tar, some boards and two spreaders that were like straightened hoes.

Lyons swung the two pails off the edge of the roof. The first missed, but the second came down on the head of an attacker. He picked up a spreader and threw it down as if he were spearing fish. His target's skull split.

He had to jump back from the edge of the roof as a burst of autofire was directed at him from below.

"Ironman."

Lyons looked up just in time to see a Sterling assault rifle coming at him end over end. He snagged it, almost losing his balance with the effort. When he recovered, Gadgets threw him a spare clip. This he caught more easily. Able Team now controlled three of the four roofs on the intersection of two laneways.

Then Lyons and Gadgets leaned over the parapets and began returning the ammunition to the terrorists. Four goons ran for the door to the tailor's shop. None of them made it.

Between the fire raining down on them from above and the approaching sirens, the terrorists' nerve broke. The retreat was even faster than the charge. Lyons and Gadgets ran out of targets before they exhausted their small supply of ammunition.

Then Flying Squad officers poured into the market, clutching handguns, shotguns and a couple of small submachine guns. Lyons and Gadgets stayed where they were until police officers came to take the Sterlings and escort them to the street.

"I MAKE THE TERRORISTS to be Bulgarian Shiites. Does that square with your findings?" Lyons asked.

Quinn chose to ignore the American's remark. "You are not obliged to answer any questions before you consult your solicitor. Do you understand?" he questioned Able Team and Babette.

"You're arresting us so the terrorists can get away. I understand perfectly," Lyons grated.

Each member of the Able Team group was seated around a couple of tables in an outdoor café in Shepherd Market. Each had a police officer watching him. Plainclothes police were keeping crowds away from the area while detectives went over everything, collecting evidence. Lyons estimated there were over a hundred policemen on the scene. Toni had already been taken to a hospital under police guard.

Quinn's stubble-covered face flushed red as he grabbed a chair at Lyons's table. He straddled it and stared at Lyons.

"There are at least seven dead men here and two more who are severely wounded. Yet you'd have me believe that you and your friends were simply out for an innocent stroll and that all of these armed terrorists attacked you. You must think we English are exceptionally gullible."

Lyons shrugged.

"Witnesses say that when shooting broke out from the roof, one of your group pulled a handgun and fired back. Is that correct?"

Lyons said nothing.

At other tables, detectives were getting no more response than Quinn managed to get from Lyons. The police inspector was thoroughly exasperated.

"Take them to Cannon Row and book them," he told a detective.

"What for, sir?"

"Firearms violations and littering. No solicitors. I don't want them talking to anyone until I get to the bottom of this."

5

David McCarter was puzzled when no one met him at the airport. When he claimed his baggage, he wasn't asked to show his firearms permit. The weapons had shown up on the routine X ray of the baggage, but McCarter simply flashed his clearance permit.

The Phoenix Force ace was solid muscle. His black polo shirt and cotton pants did nothing to hide his physique. His brown hair was still rumpled from sleeping on the plane, and his eyes flickered as if they were too hot to remain one color.

He stood in the airport with his battered bag at his feet, watching the crowd. He lit a cigarette while considering his next step. Somebody from Able Team should have met him. If no one was here, it meant something was amiss. He ducked into a washroom. When he emerged, his Browning Hi-Power rode in soft shoulder leather, two SAS concussion grenades nestled in one jacket pocket and a spare thirteen-round magazine rode in the other.

McCarter took a taxi to his own apartment in the Plaistow district. Since Able Team hadn't met him, he considered it foolish to barge in on trouble while carrying a suitcase in one hand. He had the taxi wait while he stowed his gear, put on an English-made suit and grabbed a newspaper. His preparations made as quickly as possible, he headed for the Intercontinental.

The morning headlines were full of a mysterious shoot-out in Shepherd Market. Seven armed terrorists had been killed, but the names of those responsible had not been released by Scotland Yard "for security reasons." The *Times* also ran a short piece on the attempted kidnapping of Uriel Isaac. When McCarter read that unarmed and unidentified Americans had foiled the attempt at the airport, he knew who'd been involved. His Able Team colleagues had been busy bastards.

No one responded when he used the house phone to call Able Team's rooms, and the desk clerk went out of his way to be uncooperative. McCarter lit a Player's and thought for a moment, then made his way to a pay phone.

When he finally got through to his friendly contact in the police department, McCarter went straight to the point. "Haleron, where are the Americans who got caught up in that Shepherd Market thing yesterday?"

"Friends of yours?"

"Too bloody right! Where are they?"

There was a long pause before Haleron said, "You don't know where you got this information."

"I don't even know who I'm talking to. What the hell's happening?"

"Inspector Quinn's holding them quiet."

"He can't do that!"

"Yes, he can. He has to submit a written report to the A/C, but we have this marvelous ruling allowing us to hold suspects incommunicado for twenty-four hours, if it means catching the rest of a gang."

"Rest of a gang? How many's the bloody fool holding?"

Haleron paused and sighed. McCarter grinned, knowing his friend already regretted having said so much.

"One woman is wounded. She's under police guard in hospital. Two other women and three men are in the Cannon Row lockup."

"What are they charged with, mate?"

"Illegal possession of firearms and littering."

"Shit. Let's have the rest of the story, Haleron."

"Rest of the story?"

"Don't get cute at this point. You wouldn't tell me all this unless something was stuck in your craw. What is it?"

Another sigh came over the wire. "I'm not on the case. All I've got is the breeze. It says your friends arrived unarmed and prevented the kidnapping of Isaac when he went to Heathrow to meet them. They definitely failed to report two weapons they took from the kidnappers. That put Quinn's nose out of joint.

"From what I hear, they were attacked in Shepherd Market. They used the handguns and managed to trade up to assault rifles. They made mincemeat of some very nasty customers. I don't think there's a jury in Britain that wouldn't pin a medal on them."

"And bloody Quinn has them locked up," McCarter finished.

"I could be wrong. It's his case. I just hear the breeze."

"You're not wrong," McCarter answered. "I know them."

"That's what I'm worried about. Some people wouldn't consider you an ideal character witness."

McCarter laughed. "Bloody Quinn isn't going to join my fan club. Maybe I'll get a chance to talk to you later on this trip."

"Don't bother. I don't associate with the likes of you."

McCarter made a mental note of his friend's attitude. Most of the force must be uneasy about Quinn's actions. McCarter grinned. Quinn smelled something unusual about Able Team and was following his instincts. A good thing for a detective to do, but this time he was going to get burned.

McCarter finished his cigarette as he planned his next move. If he wanted his money, he'd better free Able Team. For that matter, if he wanted to keep Able Team alive, it would be better if they weren't sitting ducks in jail.

He strode out of the hotel and hailed another taxi. As he climbed in, he noticed a sturdy woman and a stocky man with Slavic cheekbones getting into the next cab in line. They'd been lounging in the hotel when he'd arrived.

"Where to?" the driver asked.

"Take me to New Scotland Yard, the long way around, mate."

"The long way around?"

"Yeah. I like the scenery."

The driver shrugged and drove north around Green Park instead of taking the shorter route to the south. McCarter waited for five minutes before looking behind.

"The other cab's still there," the driver told him. "I'm not going to play cops and robbers, but I'll drive around a couple of blocks if you want to make sure."

McCarter leaned back. "Make sure," he told the driver.

Five minutes later the driver said, "They're still following."

McCarter had to fight the temptation to cut the taxi off and try to force answers from the car's two passengers. It would be satisfying, but the risk wasn't worth the probable results. It was his job to free Able Team, not to get himself locked up. He had no way of knowing if the pair tailing him were police.

"Take the shortest route to the Yard," McCarter told the driver, deciding that if the people following him were connected to Able Team's problems, it wouldn't hurt to let them think he was connected with Scotland Yard.

The driver cut through St. James's Park and delivered him to the modern concrete-and-glass building in five minutes. McCarter threw him a bill, jumped out of the car and took the concrete steps three at a time. At the reception desk he demanded to see Quinn.

"Your name, please. And what's it regarding?" the uniformed man asked politely.

"McCarter. Kidnapping."

After a minute on the telephone, the man behind the desk told McCarter, "Detective Inspector Quinn's busy, sir. He's sending Detective Sergeant Murphy to talk to you."

McCarter held back his temper and waited.

Murphy turned out to be a balding man of average height. He sized McCarter up with shrewd gray eyes before asking, "You said something about kidnapping?"

"Right. American friends of mine. Attacked twice by armed men, then taken and detained illegally by Detective Inspector Quinn. I want to swear charges."

"You're serious," Murphy decided.

"Damned right I'm serious. Either Quinn is charged or I go talk to a chum at Associated Press."

"You'd better come with me, sir."

McCarter shook his head. "I'll stay within sight of the entrance."

Murphy smiled. "We don't kidnap people at the Yard."

McCarter turned on his heel and strode toward the glass doors.

"Then you don't mind if I tell the American press what I know."

He reached the door before Murphy answered, "I think you'd better speak to Detective Inspector Quinn, sir."

McCarter turned slowly, warily.

"I tried that. He sent you. You deal with it."

"Exactly what do you want, sir?"

McCarter admired the other man's coolness. A smear like this would be hard on Scotland Yard. The detectives were between a rock and a hard place. Something was wrong, but they didn't know what and they had little opportunity to probe.

"My friends. I want them free or charged in twenty minutes."

"That's a solicitor's job, sir."

"A solicitor would let you hold them for twenty-four hours. I won't."

"Perhaps if Inspector Quinn came here to talk to you?"

"I'll be outside. This place stinks of cover-up." McCarter looked at his watch. "It's five to eleven. I'll leave the front steps to find a pay phone at a quarter past."

He strode out the door before Murphy could reply. The police sergeant couldn't figure what the hell was up. All he could do was pass along McCarter's threat.

Five minutes later Quinn's massive form moved down the steps to where McCarter was sitting.

"Are you Mr. McCarter?"

"That's right. You Quinn?"

The inspector went on down the steps and turned to face McCarter, who hadn't bothered to stand up.

"What can you tell me about Mr. Lyons and his friends?" Quinn asked.

"You intend to charge them with being alive?"

Quinn waved a huge hand, brushing the question aside.

"I know they're dangerous. I also know they're in danger. I'm just keeping them safe until the commissioner looks into deportation."

"It won't work, mate. They did nothing but defend themselves."

"You don't know that."

"I know them."

"Such upright citizens don't shoot to kill."

"Bullshit!"

There was a moment's silence. McCarter lit another cigarette. He didn't offer Quinn one.

"Just what do you do for a living, Mr. McCarter?"

"You don't have the security clearance to know. You tried checking. What did they tell you?"

Quinn smiled. "No one has the security clearance to know. You have a permit to carry weapons. You work for the Americans. You come and go with a suitcase full of arms, which I assume are job-related."

McCarter shrugged.

"If I let them loose, how many more people die?"

"I guess as many as try to cash them in."

"You're bluffing," Quinn decided.

"Want to try me?" the Phoenix Force commando growled.

"How did you know we had them?"

McCarter took another drag on his Player's.

"If they're set free, how do I know there won't be more trouble?"

"For you, you mean?"

Quinn made an impatient gesture. "That shooting war took place in Shepherd Market. A lot of people could have been killed. I don't want that sort of thing happening again."

"Talk to the terrorists."

"I'll have them released. Do you want to come and collect them?"

"Where are they?"

"Cannon Row."

"You providing transport?"

Quinn nodded.

"Who was wounded?"

"The woman called Toni Blancanales."

"You leave people at their hotel?"

Quinn's eyes narrowed speculatively. "Why?"

"I was followed from there."

Quinn took several minutes to think over the implications of McCarter's statement. "So there's bound to be more trouble. Why tell me?"

"You made a big mistake. I've got no reason to make your life easy. You should be pinning a medal on them."

Quinn made a face. "Vigilantes."

"No. Professionals."

Quinn nodded and turned back to the building to order cars and drivers.

POLITICIAN SAT BESIDE his sister in Grey Coat Hospital. Toni was propped up in bed, the shoulder bandage making a bulge under the striped flannel gown the hospital had provided for her. Over the gown, her left arm was in a sling.

"How bad is it?" Toni asked. "The doctors here are so noncommittal I could kick them."

"You lost a chunk of muscle. You came within a half inch of losing the ball game. That means you're in for at least six months of physiotherapy, but you'll be back in harness in two weeks and wondering why you didn't make a bigger thing out of it to get more time off."

Toni smiled. She had been brutally attacked and raped years ago. Mack Bolan and Rosario had hunted down the psychopath and helped to put her on the road to recovery. But she'd responded by becoming a workaholic. The last thing in the world she wanted was time off—time to wonder what she was doing with her life.

"Where's everyone else?" she asked.

"Waiting for me so we can have lunch. Then we're going to have to reintroduce ourselves to the terrorists."

"I want to see Carl."

"You still on his case, little sister?"

Toni shook her head. "He was right. I didn't take the danger seriously enough. I owe him an apology."

"He won't want it."

She looked puzzled and hurt.

Politician explained. "He figures people do the best they can with the knowledge they have. He's got no time for anyone who apologizes for doing what he, or she, thought was right."

"So what do I say to him?"

"How about, 'Thanks for the lift'?"

Toni smiled. "That I will say. But what about the way he does things? He isn't exactly a great salesman."

"You'd be surprised. I want to turn him loose at Quartermaster."

"They're a big account. Our reputation in the United Kingdom rests on how we handle this."

Pol smiled. "Then I leave the choice up to you. I can take charge and do my diplomatic best. Or I can let Carl take charge and be sure that we've done our best by Quartermaster."

"You and Hermann keep underrating yourselves. You're good."

Pol shook his head. "We're not good. We're terrific. But we're part of a team. The team is a hell of a lot more than the sum of its parts."

Toni patted her brother's hand. "Use your judgment."

"Uh, the police are going to continue to hang around."

"I suspected I'd need a guard. What made them let you go, by the way?"

"McCarter blackmailed Scotland Yard."

"What?"

"He threatened them with headlines like, 'Americans Jailed for Not Being Killed by British Terrorists.'"

"How badly is Able Team compromised?"

Pol shrugged. "We won't know until we're out of this. I've got the feeling the enemy knows exactly who we are." He paused and looked at his watch. "I have to go. McCarter is taking us on an information-gathering tour this afternoon."

"What does that mean?"

"I didn't ask."

"That's what I was afraid of. Take care."

McCarter walked the members of Able Team, Lao Ti and Babette Pavlovski around London until each one had mentioned pointedly that he or she hadn't intended to take a sight-seeing tour.

"That's what guides are for," McCarter replied cheerfully. Finally satisfied they weren't being followed, McCarter led his tour down Grosvenor Road, just south of the Intercontinental Hotel, and turned into a bicycle shop named Spokes Unlimited.

"Don't get Ironman another bicycle," Gadgets pleaded. "Once he gets on one of those things, there's no stopping him."

It was a rambling shop filled with bicycles and parts of bicycles. Lyons looked around with a glint of interest.

"Down, boy," McCarter told him. "That's not the sort of machine we need right now."

The man who made his way forward between the bicycles looked about as safe as a mother grizzly separated from her cub. He stood six foot five. Most of his face was hidden behind a thick black beard. A high forehead, a long straight nose and green eyes were framed by disorderly black hair.

"Hello, Felix," McCarter greeted the giant.

"Do I know you?" Felix Holmes asked.

"We're clean, and I'll vouch for these disreputable characters," McCarter assured him.

Felix broke into a grin and wrapped his hand around McCarter's. "Good to see you, David. I suppose you're here to visit the hardware section."

He led the way to the back of the store. The group passed a young man with a red beard who looked just as ferocious as the owner.

"Watch the shop!" Holmes boomed at him as the group went by.

The young man nodded silently and moved toward the front of the shop.

Holmes stopped in front of a closet door. He opened it to reveal shelves of tools. Hiding his actions from the group, the store owner did something to the cupboard. It swung open, giving access to a staircase leading down into a basement.

Holmes started to turn around when he felt a hand with a grip like a vise close on the back of his neck.

"Show your hands empty before you turn around," Lyons growled.

Holmes was unperturbed. "A cautious gentleman. I like that." He swung his hands away from his sides so those behind could see they were empty. "You don't mind if I employ similar caution and ask you to proceed downstairs."

Lyons shrugged and led the way.

The basement was an arms storehouse. Shelving was piled with small arms and parts. Larger weapons stood in racks.

Cases of explosives and ammunition stood in another aisle. Everything was arranged in neat rows, like a supermarket.

"Automatic weapons on the left. Submachine guns and related subjects on the right. Handguns, shotguns and other items are at the back of the room." Felix had obviously recited the spiel many times.

"Stock seems to have turned over since I was here last," McCarter commented. "You had British Sterlings, French MATs, a few M-16s and a lot of H&Ks then."

"Can't expect a businessman not to turn over his inventory, now can you?" Holmes rumbled. "What did you gentlemen have in mind?"

Lyons had wandered to the back of the room and was poking around. Gadgets and Lao were occupied with subguns. Babette was checking out the assault rifles. That left Politician and McCarter to do the negotiating.

"We need something we can conceal, we need firepower and we need quality for the six of us. And we need it at a price we can afford."

Holmes shook his massive head. "Quality costs money."

"How much money?"

"Depends on the demand," Holmes replied easily. "I'm just a businessman out to make a living. High demand puts the price up."

McCarter was more attuned to Holmes's thinking. The Phoenix Force hotshot asked, "Does that mean you've got some quality goods on low demand?"

"I'm afraid it does. Take a look at these."

He led the group to a pile of wooden cases and rummaged inside one until he brought out something wrapped in oiled paper, which he carefully removed. Producing a hand towel from a nearby shelf, he wiped the weapon and then his hands before passing the gun to Politician.

"Now there's superb quality no one will buy from me. I'm overstocked."

Politician leaned his cane against a stack of cases and accepted the plastic weapon. It weighed eight pounds and looked like a toy spacegun. All the parts that showed were plastic, except the trigger and the safety.

While Politician breached the weapon, Holmes remarked casually, "Speaking of unwanted but quality weapons, I could certainly sell you a better *jo* than that walking stick. And for less than you paid I bet."

"You sell martial arts equipment?"

"Not as a habit, sir, but a shipment of arms manufactured by the Chinese happened to fall into my hands. Some martial arts items were among it."

He ambled away while Politician continued to check out the weapon.

Politician called to Lyons, "Our friend has a large supply of Heckler & Koch G-11 caseless rifles. The sample he handed me is definitely new. He says he's having trouble moving them."

"It's only 4.7 mm," Lyons complained.

Holmes returned with what looked like a walking stick in his hands. He handed it to Politician, who took some appreciative swipes with it.

The gun dealer turned to Lyons. "Perfectly right, sir, but they'll penetrate a steel helmet at five hundred yards."

"How much?" Lyons asked, taking the weapon from Pol.

"It's unfortunate the soldiers of fortune and other adventurers always prefer something they've used before. Normally, for this quality of goods, I could easily get five hundred pounds each. Unfortunately, no one wants this advanced assault weapon that uses bullets without shells."

"The price," Lyons interrupted.

"Six G-11s and two hundred kilos of ammunition in disposable packs—two thousand pounds."

"All new?"

Holmes nodded.

"They're too long to carry," Gadgets objected. "Those babies are thirty inches long. That's two and a half feet, and a quick trip to the cop shop the first time you try to walk down the street.''

"Ah, yes," Holmes said. "I nearly forgot. The price also includes six memberships in the Almost Celtics Football Club.''

"The what?''

"An amateur group." Holmes dodged over three aisles and picked up a sports bag. The side of the bag bore the legend ALMOST in inch-high letters and the CELTICS in four-inch-high letters. "Zipper goes right over the end of the bag for hasty extraction of, ah, sporting paraphernalia.''

Pol looked at Lyons, then nodded.

"Very good. What else, gentlemen?''

"Over here." Lyons led the way to the rear of the arms storeroom. "How much for this?" He held up a large piece of stainless-steel plumbing.

"Ah, the Wildey. A formidable weapon, sir.''

"How long is the barrel on that thing?" Gadgets exclaimed. "Looks like an entire hot water system.''

"The barrels are interchangeable, although the longer barrels are preferred. That's the ten-inch barrel. They go down to five inches, but ten is the connoisseur's choice. A three-inch grouping at fifty yards.''

"That before or after modifications?" Lyons asked.

"Look at the dense chrome on the slide and the rounded follower in the magazine. I assure you, this version is practically trouble-free.''

"I like it," Lyons said. "No assault shotguns?''

"Unfortunately I just can't get enough. If you'd care to wait, I—''

"We're in a hurry," Lyons told him.

After much negotiating, Lyons got his Wildey, spare clips and extra .45s. The rest took Steyr GB-80s that used 9 mm parabellums, the same ammunition used in McCarter's Browning. The Wildey, four GB-80s, four spare clips a piece, soft leather rigs and extra ammunition jacked up the bill. In a burst of unbusinesslike generosity, Holmes threw in Pol's *jo*.

"Where do you want the goods delivered?" Holmes asked.

"This is cash-and-carry," Pol answered.

Holmes smiled and shook his head.

Pol looked at McCarter for an explanation.

"He doesn't let customers have both the guns and the ammunition while they're on the premises," McCarter explained. "He figures some of them would then be in a position to ask for a refund without returning the weapons."

"Stated like a gentleman," Holmes concurred.

"Deliver them to us at the Intercontinental Hotel," Lyons instructed. "Just make sure we're there."

"Aren't you going to need a new base?" McCarter asked.

Lyons shook his head. "Don't want to make it too difficult for those terrorists to find us. We'd have a hell of a time finding them."

"Too bloody right," McCarter muttered. "No wonder someone has to bail you out now and then."

Able Team took the ribbing in humble silence as Pol paid Holmes.

THE FLIGHT ACROSS THE ATLANTIC had given Aya Jishin an opportunity to contemplate the coming meeting. She looked around the boardroom table. No one was late; no one dared to be late. She called the meeting to order.

"This new location is satisfactory."

She scowled at the blank look on several faces.

Her new financial backers had discovered the ultimate source from which to recruit ruthless terrorists. Bulgaria had been doing Russia's dirty work for years, but the exploitation of Bulgaria's Muslim population had just begun. Recently the Russians had begun using the Shiite faction of the Bulgarian Muslims as storm troopers in their clandestine war against the West.

The Shiites, after years of oppression, suddenly found themselves armed and launched upon a jihad that ensured paradise for each terrorist.

The Japanese terrorist leader knew any group that had been oppressed for years became especially ruthless when power was finally achieved. The Bulgarians were supposed to be fully trained terrorists, but she doubted if the group seated before her could achieve her objectives. To begin with, their limited English made communication a source of continual frustration.

"Who set the business up?" Jishin rasped.

A studious-looking woman with horn-rim glasses and untidy red hair stood up. Her business suit and severe white blouse were the right uniform, but the cheap material already looked wrinkled.

"Your name?"

"Selma Doon."

"You are American?"

The woman nodded.

"Why are you with us?"

Selma Doon removed her glasses; she obviously chewed on the end pieces of the frames. Without glasses, her blue eyes looked watery and weak.

"I have an MBA. I want to destroy a system that condones sexual harassment in the workplace."

Jishin darted her black eyes around the table. The idea that anyone would care to harass Doon had brought smiles to some lips. Under Jishin's lightning glance, the smiles quickly withered.

"This location you chose. This is just a small town. Will people believe we manufacture high-tech parts from this location?"

Doon nodded. "They'll believe it as long as no one gets inside to see that our industrial space is really being used for barracks. Route 128 is known as High-Tech Highway, and Danvers is the most progressive of the smaller centers around Boston. The spot is a cost-per-square-foot-times-transport wonder. The potential work force is good. In short, it's the best location I could find for a company engaged in the manufacture and distribution of computer components. Provisions for your army will come in as raw materials. When you wish to make a raid, the transport trucks will look like our shipments. Everyone will believe it's a fully operational plant.''

"How much did the telephone installers see?"

"An empty building. I had the telephones installed first. Then I bought out a bankrupt travel agency, had their telephone number transferred here, used their furniture and paid off their debts so there'd be no questions.''

"You have thought things through well. Now, can you follow orders to the letter?'' Jishin asked.

Doon bit her lower lip as she nodded.

"Buy yourself a couple of expensive suits, ones that make you look like an executive and not a shopgirl. If anyone asks, you are the general manager here. What are we calling this outfit?''

"Central Dynamics. I've already ordered stationery and a sign.''

"Good. If you have any trouble with your front staff, you are to tell Yoru immediately. He handles discipline.''

Doon looked at the squat Japanese in the English business suit before nodding in agreement. Yoru grinned at her, the sort of grin a shark reserves for a large school of plump fish.

"Now that that's all settled, we must make up for a setback encountered in England. We had three objectives over there. First, to raise money. Two companies paid up enough to supplement the money put in by our backers.

"Second, we needed to establish a base in England long enough to get our main body of troops into the United States. By hiring them from our own high-tech firm over there, we actually got visas and work permits.

"The final objective was to come away with a third-generation advanced computer. We have not yet succeeded."

She paused to glance around the table before continuing. "We should still manage to get software for the new chip Megatronics so thoughtfully donated. But I believe in covering all contingencies."

She paused again. Many of the Bulgarians were obviously not following her speech.

"We need a Cray computer. We make our first hit tomorrow," Jishin shouted.

A number of the terrorists nodded their understanding.

6

Able Team, McCarter, Lao Ti and Pavlovski had kept an eye on their hotel from positions outside of it. If the terrorists appeared, Able Team wanted to spot them, but without weapons they didn't want to be inside where the opportunities for evasion were limited.

They watched Felix Holmes arrive with four husky men. Holmes carried the sports bags holding the weapons. Each of the other men carried a heavy cardboard carton labeled Harrods Fine China. Handle With Care.

Able Team watched the hotel for five minutes before returning inside. They found Holmes and his friends waiting outside the room shared by Pol and Ironman.

Once inside the room, Holmes said, "Here you are, gentlemen. Same-day delivery. How's that for service?"

"Quality," Politician said.

Holmes beamed.

"It's been a pleasure, gentlemen."

"You're satisfied with the transaction?" Lyons said, his voice cracking like a whip.

"Reasonably," Holmes answered warily.

"Then we have another piece of business."

"I was afraid it would come to this."

The gunrunner's statement was a signal to his four men. They each produced a Steyr GB-80 with the smooth, economical motion of professionals.

Pol's stick whished in a blur. Two of the automatics went flying. Gadgets's ax-hand thrust sent a gun crashing to the floor. Lyons hadn't taken his eyes from Holmes, but a side kick sent the last weapon flying.

There was a moment's silence as the stricken gunmen looked toward Holmes for instructions. None of them had made the mistake of diving after his weapon.

Holmes sighed. "Let's have it."

"I didn't see any Webley Mark 1s in your stock," Lyons snapped. "Either you didn't supply the group trying to kill us or you sold them your entire stock. Which?"

"I've got a few Sterlings, but other than that I seldom handle British weapons. The manufacturers keep good books. They know who buys their guns. I have the Sterlings from an army auction. Got a legit front who bids and makes out phony export papers. The guns used on you were never mine, sir."

"Then who supplied them?"

"How should I know?" Holmes rumbled.

"You're a businessman. Don't tell us you don't know your competition," Politician said gently.

"And do you know what happens to businessmen who tell stories about their competitors?" Holmes asked.

"Okay," Lyons told the gunrunner. "You can go."

Holmes looked puzzled. It was too easy. He signaled his disarmed guards to proceed him out the door.

"Hold it!" Lyons barked.

They froze.

"I said you go," Lyons said, scooping up one of the Steyrs. "These guys pulled guns on us. They're gone."

The rest of Able Team picked up the goons' weapons. McCarter pulled out his Browning. The silence in the room was a balanced jar of nitroglycerin. Holmes seemed ready to face personal threat, but his face told Able Team he didn't dare let it be known he'd walked out on four of his men, leaving them to be killed.

"There's only two possibilities," Holmes said in a small voice. "Punk named Pawley runs a hockshop in Soho. He dabbles in AWOL shooters. The other toolroom is Helen's Tea Company."

"What?"

McCarter cut in. "One of the suppliers to the IRA, mate. I know about Helen."

Each member of Able Team removed the clip from the weapon he was holding and tossed the Steyrs back to their owners.

"Thanks for the extra clips," Lyons told Holmes.

"Not to mention it."

"Don't worry. Your name won't come up. Hope we do business again sometime."

"Not unless I have the bleedin' army standing behind me," Holmes muttered as he led his helpers out and vanished down the hall.

"You're worse at making friends than I am," McCarter observed.

Lyons ignored him. He checked all the bags until he found the one containing the Wildey and spare clips. He put the shoulder leather over his bulletproof suit and tested the ride and draw of the gun. Then he joined the rest in degreasing and checking the G-11s.

In fifteen minutes everyone was ready to go again. They carefully closed up the open cases of ammunition and stacked them in the closet. Then each shouldered an Almost Celtics sports bag and headed back to the stairs.

"You guys ever hear about elevators?" McCarter complained.

"Yeah. Those are the cages where they keep cutting the power between floors or someone waits on a lower floor for the doors to open so he can toss in a grenade. Those the contraptions you mean?" Gadgets answered.

"You birds are positively paranoid," McCarter grumbled.

"Just because you're paranoid..." Lyons began.

"Doesn't mean they're not out to get you." Gadgets, Pol and Lao Ti finished the sentence for him.

"Bloody bunch of lunatics, that's what I've got," McCarter grumbled as he followed the rest down seven flights of stairs.

Able Team didn't worry that McCarter was in tail position. They knew he was as watchful as they were.

When they'd reached the sidewalk, Lyons said, "First, we get our suits. Then we split up."

"No you don't, man," Gadgets contradicted. "First, we get our threads, then we eat. After that you can make decisions."

The six of them walked in pairs through the southern tip of Mayfair: Gadgets and Babette, Politician and Lao, Lyons and McCarter. Periodically the lead pair would pause and look around as the other four walked by.

"It's like being on a sight-seeing tour for loonies," McCarter muttered as he systematically checked rooftops.

While he and Lyons were scanning buildings and the rest walked by, the two men were approached by a short, wiry young man.

"The Almost Celtics. Is that amateur football?"

Lyons almost said, "Not football, soccer," but caught himself. His hesitation gave McCarter time to field the question.

"Right, mate. You play?"

"I'm the fastest right wing around," the young man told them in his modest fashion.

"But do you pass?" McCarter asked.

Lyons took a few more steps and stopped, still scanning the street.

"Sure. I'm a team player."

"Not the ball. This is no sissy league. We pass the opposition."

"What d'yer mean?"

"Like this. Heads up, Ironman."

Lyons looked around to discover that McCarter had seized the young man by the waist and heaved him bodily. The soccer player was headed at Lyons like a torpedo. Lyons wrapped his left arm around the kid. His right hand grabbed the man's belt and slung him back. He went flying back to McCarter.

David caught the Londoner's wrists, swung him around once and set him on his feet.

"See, mate? Now, let's see you do it to me. Toss me over to the big guy."

The small footballer eyed McCarter's six feet of muscle and backed away as if he expected the Phoenix Force warrior to throw him around again. Then the small man turned and gave a fine display of open-field running.

"See," McCarter said as he and Lyons strode to catch up to the rest, "don't hurt to be sociable now and then."

The businesses in Shepherd Market had made a quick recovery from the major battle of the previous day. Window glass had been replaced, all the shops were open and the owners were eager to wait on the crowds who'd come to gawk at the site of the minor war.

McCarter insisted they wait until he went into a corner store for a cold Coke Classic to guzzle as they continued to the tailor's shop. He emerged pouring the contents of a liter bottle down his throat.

This time the approach went like a military maneuver. McCarter and Lao stopped at the downstairs door and eyed the crowds. Babette stationed herself outside the second-floor door to Joc's shop. Lyons, Schwarz and Blancanales entered cautiously, their eyes darting around, failing to detect signs of the enemy on the premises.

"I was expectin' ye a might earlier," Joc said as he emerged from the back room.

Politician grinned. "Weren't you afraid we might not turn up?"

"Nae. I watched from the window. I wouldn't a bought daytime suits if ye needed them for yer coffins."

There was no answer to Joc's practical approach, so the men stripped off their jackets and pants to be fitted.

Joc's assistant hurried to place a chair by each man.

"Put yer weapons on the backs of the chairs and remove yer shirts and socks," the tailor ordered. "I certainly wasn't going to trust ye to buy yer own accessories after I chose yer suits."

Smiling, the three warriors did as directed, ignoring the shop assistant who collected the clothing they'd just removed.

They were handed dress shirts. Gadgets's and Pol's showed a hairline stripe. Ironman's was a soft yellow. Each received a plain tie and matching socks. They quickly put them on. Joc knocked Lyons's hands away from his dull yellow tie. The little tailor tied it to his satisfaction, then handed Ironman his underarm rig.

Pol and Gadgets were each given vests to put on before they donned their holstered Steyrs. The pants came next. The tailor checked the fit of the waist and hips.

"Hey," Politician protested, "I can't tell if the pants are the right length without my shoes."

Joc's voice was frosty. "I measured them meself. They're correct. Yer shoes will be back in a few minutes."

They had no time to think about the shoes because the tailor put them through a series of calisthenics designed to test the fit of the pants.

"When I looked out the window and saw how active you gentlemen can be, I took the liberty of adding a fine silk lining to the trousers," Joc told them.

The jackets took more time to fit. With actual gun leather strapped in place, the tailor insisted on adjusting each seam until the jackets fell smoothly without giving a hint of the extra space under the arms.

The assistant returned with three pair of shoes. The scuff marks had been dyed, and the leather had been buffed to a dull, soft shine.

"Incredible," Pol said as he gazed in the mirror. "Best suit I've had. Don't believe it's off the rack."

"I suspect it isn't by now," Gadgets remarked.

Pol's conservative gray suit had a fine pinstripe. There was a flair that American tailoring hadn't provided. It made him look his age. Most of his expensive suits left him looking considerably older.

Gadgets's suit was a medium blue, solid tone.

"It should have been brown," Joc lamented.

Lyons was given a blue Harris Tweed jacket to go with gray flannel slacks, yellow shirt and darker yellow tie.

"Sharp," he told the mirror.

Joc shuddered.

While Pol paid the tailor, the assistant packed spare shirts and socks and Able Team's old clothing into flat boxes with cardboard handles. Politician looked at the additional baggage and arranged to have it sent to the hotel.

Babette was the first to see the new clothes. Carefully keeping her face deadpan, she said to Gadgets, "Pardon me, sir. Have you seen my three scruffy friends who went in there half an hour ago?"

"Sorry, old thing," Gadgets replied in an atrocious British accent. "They walked in and dived straight out the windows. Must have wanted to get away from someone."

"Just as well. Mind if I take up with you then?"

"I don't know," Gadgets told her. "How are you with a clothes brush?"

"If you're that kinky, forget it," Babette said.

Gadgets could keep a straight face no longer and exploded into laughter.

McCarter's comments were different. "If I knew you needed a guide just so you could dress like a bunch of stuffed shirts, I'd have stayed at home."

"You are at home," Lyons reminded him as he led the way to the sidewalk café.

It gave Lyons a sense of satisfaction to sit and order supper at the table where the police had interrogated him the day before. None of the merchants from yesterday gave the group a second glance.

"All right," Lyons said as he sipped a watery cup of British coffee after the meal. "We split up. Gadgets, you, Lao and Babette get into Quartermaster and see if you can trace the bug pickups. I'll take Pol and the English nut and see if we can get more information from Pawley or Helen."

THE ONLY PEOPLE at Quartermaster Software when Gadgets, Babette and Lao arrived were Isaac, Zimmerman and the night security staff. The only indication that the company was under siege was the lack of cleaning staff.

"I see Joc took care of you," Isaac remarked.

Gadgets grinned. "He's together, man."

"I trust that's satisfactory," the puzzled industrialist replied.

As the general manager and chairman of the board watched, Gadgets and Lao started to trace the wires that led away from each bug. They worked in determined silence while Babette watched their backs. It was evident they trusted no one until they knew more about who and what they were up against.

Isaac and Zimmerman watched for a while, then returned to the boardroom, which was the only area they knew was clean, to continue their discussions.

PAWLEY'S PROPER PAWNSHOP WAS on Shaftesbury and occupied one building in a row of connected, narrow, three-story structures. The store was locked, steel grating pulled over both the doorway and the display window. The night light showed that no one was in the shop.

"Light on the top floor," Lyons said.

Lyons, Blancanales and McCarter continued their slow stroll past the store without breaking pace. They crossed the street at the corner and wandered back the other way, then crossed back and walked around the row of buildings to see if the upstairs could be reached without going through the pawnshop. But they couldn't find any indication of such an entrance.

"How'll we get up there?" McCarter asked.

"The roof and rope," Lyons answered.

"Shit. I knew you'd say that. It's a good thing we don't have rope."

"Pol, that's your department."

"Let's wander over a couple of streets into the residential section," Politician suggested.

They strolled down a dark street of small houses until Pol said, "Wait."

He walked up to a front door and knocked. The door opened less than an inch. Politician stood on the small front stoop, leaning on his cane and smiling, as if he were visiting an old friend. The door closed again, but Pol didn't move.

"He looks too toff for this area," McCarter remarked.

The door opened again. Politician exchanged a bank note for a paper bag and came down the walk whistling.

"What did you pay for it?" McCarter demanded.

"Five pounds."

"For a few pence worth of rope! You're daft. Anyone can walk down the street, spot a clothesline, then pay the owner a ridiculous amount for it. But as soon as the police ask questions, the guy will run forward with the answers damn fast."

"You're right," Politician agreed happily.

"Then why did you do it?"

"I didn't. When I spotted the clothesline I wanted, I went to a neighbor and offered to buy his nonexistent clothesline."

There was a moment of silence before McCarter burst into laughter. "If I ever decide on a life of crime, I'll know who to look up," the Briton gasped.

One store in the row with the pawnshop had a fire escape, leading to an easy distance from the roof. The three warriors crept up the metal steps. Lyons boosted Pol to the roof, where he tied off the rope for the other two to climb.

The walk over the rooftops was only two hundred yards, but it took the trio ten minutes. Many of the roofs sloped steeply, the heights not matching, and they moved cautiously, not wanting those underneath to hear their footfalls.

They found a stout chimney in direct line with the lit window over the pawnshop. Once the rope was secure, Lyons removed his jacket, then dangled the rope over the eaves to measure the drop to the window.

As he adjusted the H&K caseless to ride on his back without catching, McCarter whispered, "Just a minute, chum. This is the sort of thing I was trained for."

"Got a coin?"

The English commando nodded.

"Flip it."

McCarter tossed it, whispering, "Call it."

As he concentrated on catching the coin lit only by streetlights two stories below, Lyons held on to the rope at a point he'd knotted and leaped backward as far as he could. By the time McCarter caught the coin, Lyons had already dropped out of sight. The rope sprang taut with Lyons ten feet out from the wall and eight feet below the rooftop. He then swung in feet first.

Lyons's shoes hit the intersections of bars between the panes and took out the entire bottom half of the window. Then he was inside, snagging his pants only once on a sliver of glass.

A short individual with a cigarette hanging from one corner of his mouth stood in the middle of the room. His long hair was slicked straight back. He needed a shave, and his white shirt was gray at the collar. However, there was nothing seedy about the Beretta SO-4 over and under shotgun that he was swinging around. Lyons didn't have a chance.

7

Lao Ti looked at Gadgets Schwarz.

He nodded. Without saying a word, they refastened the meter to the panel in the basement of Quartermaster Software. Then they quietly picked up their tools and returned to the boardroom.

"Time for a late stroll," Gadgets told Uriel Isaac and Nate Zimmerman.

The two Quartermaster executives looked at each other, then Isaac shrugged. Without questions or any argument, the two men went to their offices for their coats, then joined Gadgets and Lao in front of the building.

Gadgets took the men on a walk that doubled back on itself and turned corners haphazardly. Lao followed a block behind, checking that no one was following. Gadgets finally led Isaac and Zimmerman to the back of their own building.

"How quickly can you get a metal semitrailer to park by that stretch of your back wall? And how long can you keep it there?" Gadgets asked.

"When do you need it and how long would you like it there?" Zimmerman countered.

"I want it as of fifteen minutes ago. If it gets in position soon enough, I want it until I can buy materials and rig an array of directional antennae on the spot. That could be as late as noon tomorrow."

"Two businesses farther up have to get by that spot to park," Isaac pointed out.

"You know any of the officers of those businesses?"

Both executives nodded.

"Get on the blower tonight and make your arrangements. But use a pay phone."

"What have you got?" Isaac wanted to know.

"The eavesdropping devices all activate a series of microrecorders. The recorders are hidden behind the panel containing the building's electric and gas meters. Lao and I examined them. The recorders are almost full. If they'd been dumped lately, the spools would be rewound."

"Dumped?" Isaac asked.

"Someone triggers the recorders to broadcast their contents, one at a time, while on fast rewind. When your terrorists have their information, the tapes are all set to record again. Activating the recorders from a remote location is called dumping. The entire mechanism is there."

"And the lorry you want?"

"Should prevent our friends from activating the dump until we're ready for them. They're not going to give us the payoff instructions until they have a chance to listen to those tapes."

Zimmerman stroked his chin. "So that means they should have dumped the recorders by now."

Gadgets nodded. "I guess they're either watching the store or cleaning you out."

"I beg your pardon?"

"It has to be someone on either your cleaning or security staff. They're waiting for a report on what's been done about the bugs we found."

The biting night wind ruffled Nate Zimmerman's dark hair and caused him to turn up the collar of his tweed overcoat. He turned to his chairman with a shrug.

"Joe will do it for us," Isaac said.

"An hour," Zimmerman told Gadgets.

"Okay," Gadgets said. "Lao and I are going back to disconnect the bugs in one lab. Find us an assistant who can spring us parts, no matter who's using them. We'll have to buy stuff when the stores open, but we need all the head start we can get.''

Isaac sighed. ''That will be myself, Mr. Schwarz. I built this business from the ground up. We have an accumulation of odd parts from breadboarding communications circuits. I should be able to come up with most of the things we need.''

''Then go and make the telephone calls. I'll do a temporary disconnect on the bugs in your basement lab. Things will be ready when you get back.''

The chairman of the board nodded briefly and strode off.

LYONS TOOK ONE LOOK at the twelve-gauge swinging around to meet him and let go of the rope. As he flew toward the gunman, his body straightened to vertical.

''Die!'' Lyons screamed.

The gunman started and yanked the trigger. Lyons was only a foot from the end of both barrels when the gun went off.

The double blast in the small room made Ironman's ears ring. Somehow he'd managed to dodge the blast, then knocked the gun out of the man's hand. ''What the fuck do you think you're doing?'' the blond commando shouted.

Pawley, pawnbroker and dealer in stolen arms, stared at the intruder. Then he jerked his eyes upward to meet the furious blue ice of Lyons's glower. Pawley's eyes rolled up, and he fainted, falling across his own coffee table.

Lyons snorted in disgust and went to stand at the broken window. The wreckage from his swinging entrance crunched under his feet. He pulled out a few shards to prevent them from falling into the street. Traffic still streamed—apparently no one had heard the commotion.

''Cities are the same everywhere,'' Lyons muttered as he gave two jerks on the rope to the roof, then grabbed the end.

McCarter slid down the rope and through the broken window. Pol was right behind him with both his and Lyons's sports bags over his shoulders.

"You smart bastard," McCarter grumbled. "You said to flip a bleedin' coin."

"Did you?" Lyons asked.

McCarter ignored the question, choosing to continue his complaints.

"You're bloody lucky there was a traffic jam on the street. You made enough noise to steal their show."

Politician stared at Ironman and the debris on the floor. "You okay?"

Lyons nodded.

"Christ! Who's he?" McCarter asked, pointing toward Pawley.

"Our friendly local pawnbroker who was waiting for us with both barrels primed."

"Hey, Ironman, we were going to question him," Politician said in a quiet voice.

"He just fainted. Take care of him while I go check this place out."

Lyons wandered out of the room to check out the top-floor apartment. He found no one else in it. There was still no reaction to the breaking window and the shotgun blast. Lyons decided that few people lived over the shops in the area. Most of the buildings had been renovated, changing dingy apartments into dingier offices. By the time he returned to the front room, Pawley had recovered. Lyons stood in the doorway behind Pawley and watched.

The dealer had been thrown into an easy chair facing the window. He started to get up, looked at McCarter and Pol standing over him, then thought better of it.

"Wot d'yer want?" He meant it to sound demanding, but he couldn't keep the whine out of his voice.

"You know what we want," McCarter told him.

"Ya take me for a bloomin' mind reader?"

"Why'd you try to kill our friend?" Pol demanded. "That toy of yours nearly blasted a hole right through him."

Pawley straightened, then collapsed back into the chair. "'E came crashin' in 'ere," the pawnbroker complained.

"And you were waiting with your finger on the trigger."

"So wot if I was? A man's got a right to defend himself, ain't 'e?"

"You were waiting. So you know why we're here. Are you going to waste any more of our time?" McCarter barked.

"Dunno wot you're talking about."

McCarter reached over the small man's head and gestured for Lyons to move behind the chair. Then he reached down and swung the easy chair so that it faced away from the broken window. "You have one more chance," the Phoenix Team warrior said.

Pawley shook his head. "Felix will know who done it. You don't dare off me."

"Nice theory." McCarter hoisted the small man out of the chair. "Last chance to grass before you take flying lessons."

"You're bluffin'."

McCarter put his hands under Pawley's arms and lifted the man as easily as if he were a child.

"I call this the shit put event," McCarter grated.

He heaved, and Pawley squawked like a chicken as he flew toward the fractured window.

Lyons caught the flailing form at the last moment and held it by one leg. Pawley tried to kick loose, so Lyons obliged by dropping him. Pawley looked up from the broken glass just inside his window. He was not at all assured to see the towering blond figure before him.

As Lyons reached down for the illegal gun trader, the small man's nerve broke. "Wot d'yer want to know?" he screeched.

Politician hastily squatted by Pawley's head, interposing his body between the man lying in the broken glass and Lyons. "You sell a batch of Mark 1s recently? They looked new."

"Dunno anything about them."

Politician stood up again. "He's lying," he told Lyons. "If he really didn't know anything, he would have said so off the top."

Lyons bent down and picked up the leg again.

"Honest, I didn't sell no Webleys. They wanted a hundred automatic shooters that all use the same ammo. I don't 'andle that sort of thing."

"How much?" McCarter asked.

"Huh?"

"How much commission did you make on the referral?"

"I dunno..." Pawley began, but he changed his tune as Lyons heaved him up by one leg and swung him toward the window. "A thousand quid."

"Only ten a shooter. You were outclassed, mate. Who?"

"I can't say. They'll kill me."

Lyons extended his arms out the window. "You can take your chances with them, or have a sure thing with us. Choose now."

"Let go," Pawley whined. Then when he realized what he'd said he began to stammer. "N-no. D-d-don't let go."

"Who?" Lyons's voice was bored, businesslike.

"'Elen," Pawley gasped. "The IRA's the only ones with that number of weapons."

"Why would they sell them?"

"'Ell, the damn Yanks ship 'em more than they could ever use."

Lyons's face grew grim, but he swung the bleating gun dealer inside. It wasn't the dealer's fault that the truth stank. Lyons dropped him back into the rubble.

"You want to live?" McCarter asked.

"I told you everything. Honest!" Pawley squeaked.

"That wasn't the question, mate. You wanna live?"

Pawley nodded.

"Then let us out of here without sounding an alarm. The police arrive, and we can't leave witnesses. We don't mind leaving you dead because you have powder on your hands. We don't."

The three warriors waited while Pawley considered his options.

"'Ow do I know you won't put one in me any'ow?"

"You don't," Lyons rumbled. "You want to take your chances or enjoy a sure thing?"

"Come on," Pawley muttered as he pulled himself to his feet.

Watched intently by all three men to make sure he triggered no alarms, the dealer in stolen weapons led them downstairs, through his pawnshop and unlocked both the front door and the steel grillwork. Then he stood there with his knees shaking.

When all three were outside, Pawley let out a nervous, "Christ! I've 'ad it."

Lyons looked back and raised an eyebrow.

"If you'd a coshed me on the way out, I'da 'oped to live. Get it over with."

"You're not worth the bother," Lyons answered. "You can't even shoot hard."

He strode away to catch up to the other two, leaving Pawley experiencing another bout of the shakes.

"What part of glamorous London do you gents want to see next?" McCarter asked.

"Helen's Tea Company."

"I was afraid you'd say that. Might not be a bad idea to include the rest of your excursion group."

"They're busy."

"Casket-fitting rooms right this way," McCarter grumbled.

HELEN'S TEA COMPANY was a dilapidated three-story brick warehouse on the Thames at Queenhithe near Southwark Bridge.

"Looks like it hasn't been used in years," Blancanales remarked.

"Always looks that way. There's no clotheslines to steal. Why don't I talk us in?"

"That'll be the night."

"Seriously, I've fought these bastards long enough to know how they think."

Lyons and Politician exchanged shrugs.

"Your play," Lyons told him.

McCarter walked to the darkened door and pushed it open. Even after the darkness of the dockside, the interior was dim.

Overhead, three forty-watt bulbs in small reflectors stabbed vainly at the Stygian blackness. A long counter ran across the room, not unlike an old stand-up bar. Four men, who were gathered at the counter thirty feet from the door, stopped and stared at the intruders.

"We're looking for Helen," McCarter said.

The beefiest of the men must have weighed in at three hundred pounds. His striped shirtsleeves were rolled up over muscular forearms. He wore a derby and a vest. No jacket. The cigar in his mouth looked like a stage prop; it was half gone but had never been lit.

"Mr. Helen to you, squirt. What you want?" the man asked in a deep, booming voice.

"He doesn't really want to know," Politician said.

Helen glanced at Politician, seemed to decide he was too small to notice and returned his attention to McCarter.

"I asked wot the hell you want."

"Guns."

"You're already carrying."

"I'm told you can supply them by the hundred."

"Who the hell told you a lie like that? Gunpowder tea I can sell you by the hundredweight, but I don't carry no weapons."

"You don't seem very worried about our weapons," Lyons said.

"I don't use 'em meself, but I've got friends," Helen said. "They dropped in when I was told to expect you gents."

"Shit," McCarter complained. "Felix sure likes to talk."

"Seems as you were the gents responsible for that. We been waiting." Helen's gesture took in the far reaches of the cavernous warehouse.

From the shadows on each side a group of men emerged, each armed with an M-16.

"Through the middle!" Lyons roared.

The three Stony Man warriors ignored the oncoming army and charged Helen and his three bodyguards. They moved in so quickly that the flankers couldn't fire without the risk of hitting their own boss.

McCarter leaped five feet and then launched a kick that sent one man to his knees, holding his crotch.

Ironman moved between the two on the giant's other side. His fist smashed into one, driving him against the long counter. His knee came up at the other, who twisted and received a pulverized thigh muscle for his trouble. The thug tried to snatch a weapon from his jacket pocket, but Lyons's hand closed over the gun hand and squeezed.

The Irishman who'd hit the counter rolled with his snub-nosed revolver clearing belt leather. Lyons snap-kicked the wrist and broke it.

The man whose hand was trapped between Lyons's hand and his own gun began to scream to accompany the music of breaking bones.

Helen looked around and found himself confronted by a small man with white hair. The American even carried a cane. The six-five gunrunner reached out with a hand like a backhoe. His favorite trick was to grab someone's face and squeeze until things began to break. This one looked fit, but not too difficult.

The stick sang a high-pitched note, and Helen's hand was knocked aside, smarting. He tried to close it into a fist. It wouldn't close. While he looked down in wonder at three broken fingers, the stick plunged into his ample gut. He bowed low, then fell on his face. He rolled to one side, fighting to catch his breath, his broken fingers forgotten.

As the thugs fell away from the three warriors, their value as protective cover decreased. The Stony Man trio had no choice but to vault the counter as autofire began to find them. They didn't stay behind the counter to be chewed up by .223 tumblers biting through the wood. Instead, they zigzagged down warehouse aisles.

The aisles were piled with wooden cases over twenty feet high. They couldn't find cross aisles. Huge mechanical lifts, each designed to stack and retrieve pallets as high as sixty feet, came from the other end of the warehouse. Their din was earsplitting. Each stacker had a driver in the cab and a gunman perched on the forks.

Each of the three, trapped in a separate aisle, turned to retreat, but the counter was lined with gunmen, set up like patrons at a shooting gallery.

8

Each of the three Stony Man warriors reacted differently to the trap they found themselves in.

McCarter ignored the threat from the sniper on the stacker. He didn't take time to yank the H&K G-11 from the sports bag. He grabbed it inside the bag, thumbed off the safety and sent a short burst along the top of the counter visible at the end of his aisle. The two-second burst hammered twenty heart-stoppers that were shared equally by four gunmen.

McCarter ran ahead of the sniper fire coming from the machine behind him, zigzagging as much as the aisle would allow.

Lyons ignored the gunmen scrambling to line up on him from behind the counter. The stainless-steel Wildey cleared leather smoothly. He took one careful shot at the gunman on the forklift. Leaving the barrel at fifteen hundred feet per second, the 230-grain .45 Magnum bullet cored the rotten apple.

The second shot entered the driver's forehead and removed the back of his skull.

Lyons practiced his broken-field running and dived behind the stacking machine just as a hail of bullets snapped down the aisle.

Politician didn't take time to go for any weapon. He still had his *jo* in his hand and his war bag on his shoulder when he sprinted straight at the threatening machine. The gunman wasn't prepared for the increasingly steep angle of firing. Bullets hit the floor a full four feet behind the white-haired warrior.

Politician charged the approaching machine. At the last moment, he lunged with his stick, thrusting it between the rails of the lift and into the eye of the grinning driver. The goon died instantly.

Pol wrapped his arms around the rails and held on until the driver's foot came off the accelerator switch. Above, the gunman thrust his M-16 through the slats of the pallet where he rode. Before he could line up, Pol swung himself into the driver's compartment. He crouched in the cab while .223s from the end of the aisle snapped around him, then pulled his G-11 from the bag and sent a short burst through the pallet. The gunman followed his M-16 to the floor sixteen feet below.

Pol got to his knees and sent a burst down the aisle. Two of the terrorists were blown away and collapsed behind the counter. A third survived by throwing himself on the floor while the other two were still shooting.

Politician pushed the driver's corpse to one corner of the tight cab, and resting his G-11 on a crossbar in front of him, pushed the electric switch to the floor. The stacker rumbled full speed ahead.

McCarter stopped suddenly and whirled. The caseless subgun tore out the end of the sports bag as it sent a shower of greetings to the sniper behind him. The sniper dropped to the floor, blood streaming down underneath him.

The driver, realizing it was suicide to keep advancing, tried to reverse the machine. But the big stacker was too slow. The 4.7 mm invitations to hell snapped right through the soft iron cab and chewed him into oblivion.

McCarter threw himself on his stomach and crawled as quickly as he could. When he was within ten feet of the edge of the aisle, two more gunners stepped up to try to win the cigar. David McCarter sent a sustained burst the length of the counter at knee height. The gunmen's screams assured him he'd found his targets.

The caseless clicked empty, and a cursing McCarter rummaged in the sports bag for two more plastic sticks of ammo, only to discover they'd fallen from the shot-up bag during his crawl and now lay spaced down the aisle behind him.

McCarter backpedaled in a hurry and retrieved two fifty-round plastic sticks. He was in the process of opening the G-11 to slam them in place when four more customers stepped up to the counter to try to knock over the wooden duck. McCarter cursed, but his hands still went on with their task of loading.

At the end of the same aisle, McCarter caught Lyons leaving his cover. The Ironman paused to throw fresh shells into the Wildey clip. He leathered the big auto and pulled his G-11 from his war bag before retreating to the far end of the aisle. When he poked his head around the back of the stacks, he came close to losing it. The air was thick with .223 tumblers as twenty more troops poured through the rear door.

Ironman threw himself to the floor with his head just past the end of the row. He held the trigger down and did two figure eights that reduced half the terrormongers to a pile of garbage. Often the 4.7 mm flesh-eaters bored right through the front rank into the man behind.

The troops who managed to survive did so by diving into aisles before the lead storm reached them. Some tried to shoot back, but most were dead before they could lower their fire to floor level. Lyons pulled his feet under him and took the back cross aisle to the next aisle.

He had just reached the aisle when a voice behind him snapped, "Freeze."

A few aisles over, Pol's stacker was rumbling at full speed. Politician was surprised to find how well the G-11 balanced for one-handed operation. A burst to the left and right each found flesh to eat. Then he saw more men coming through the front door. He didn't know if they were friends or enemies, but he wasn't going to wait around to find out. He threw the stacker in reverse, packed the corpse on the accelerator and swung himself off the machine to beat it to the back of the warehouse.

McCarter couldn't figure out why the thugs at the end of the aisle weren't shooting. He slammed the G-11 closed just as three SAS men appeared holding Sterling subguns on the four at the counter. The criminals set down their weapons carefully and raised their hands.

When everything was safe, a six-foot-three officer with a long face and pinched cheeks stepped to the counter and grinned down at McCarter on the floor.

"Give me one good reason why I shouldn't let these gentlemen pick up their weapons and continue their target practice," Major Simms barked.

McCarter stood up, keeping the G-11 in his hand.

"Because you don't have the guts to do it in front of witnesses," McCarter answered.

The bushy gray-brown eyebrows furrowed together in a frown.

"I've just saved your ass, McCarter. Now drop the weapon."

"No. If I was disarmed, *you* would shoot."

The pale green eyes burned with hatred. "You're under arrest, McCarter. You and your half-assed friends. Now drop it."

"What's the charge, Simms?"

"Major Simms to you."

"I'm no longer under your command. I don't have to put up with that shit from an incompetent."

Simms addressed the four SAS troopers holding guns to the heads of the four hardmen. "Jones, remove the prisoners. The rest of you cover this idiot. If he doesn't drop the gun on the count of three, fire."

At the far end of the same aisle, Ironman held his weapon out to the side, muzzle up. He was puzzled by being told to freeze. The opposition hadn't seemed interested in taking prisoners. Normally he would have whirled and fired, hoping his flak jacket would help him survive the odds, rather than surrendering to a certain and prolonged death. But some instinct held him back.

"You have two seconds to identify yourself," Lyons said over his shoulder. He noticed that all firing had stopped—his first solid clue that he was dealing with the law.

The authority in Lyons's voice and his indifference to the guns trained on him caught his captors by surprise.

"Lieutenant Forbes, SAS, supporting CID. Now put down the weapon," the squad leader barked.

Lyons did so. The grim-faced SAS troopers gestured him toward the front of the building. Lyons walked up the aisle, his hands in the air and six guns aimed at his back. He came up behind McCarter, who still held his G-11. The Phoenix Force warrior stood sneering at a flush-faced officer on the other side of the counter.

"They're not going to shoot, Simms. They know me. They know what an idiot you are. Shove it."

"One," Simms began.

Lyons calmly walked past McCarter, placing himself between McCarter and the angry major.

"Get out of the way!" Simms shouted.

Ironman kept coming, his hands in the air.

Politician reached the end of his aisle just in time to see the SAS troops disappearing into the next aisle. He recognized the fatigues, even in the dim light of the warehouse. He looked down the row and realized that Ironman had been taken prisoner. There was no way Able Team could afford to be booked on weapons charges. Running fast and silently, he closed in on the SAS troops.

He brought his *jo* up and swung it against the temple of the first soldier. He went down without a sound.

The second blow only stunned the tough SAS commando, who bellowed and turned. Politician put him out of action by swinging his G-11 into the guy's jaw, but three more soldiers were spinning, fingers already tightening on triggers. Pol kept plowing forward, although he knew he was about to be blasted. There was no way he'd fire back at soldiers on the same side.

Lyons used Pol's distraction to walk straight toward the bullet-wrecked counter. The SAS stepped to either side, trying to keep a line of fire on McCarter. To their dismay, they found a solid wall of their own men behind the fiery-tempered antiterror expert.

Simms was the only person who held his position behind the counter.

"Halt!" he ordered.

Lyons halted, after he'd reached the counter.

"Are you in charge?" he demanded.

"I'm commanding the SAS forces. We're assisting CID. Now put your hands behind you to be cuffed."

Lyons started to lower his hands, then rammed them forward, grabbing the jacket of the surprised Simms. Before Simms could call out, he was dragged across the counter as a human shield for Lyons and McCarter.

When McCarter realized that Lyons's actions had committed them to action, he ducked and swung his G-11 back. The stock knocked a Sterling toward the ceiling just as a nervous finger squeezed the trigger. The roof was decorated with a pattern of 5.56 mm holes.

McCarter kicked another soldier to one side and then slammed his fist into the side of the first SAS trooper's head before he could bring his deadly subgun back to target acquisition.

Lyons saw one trooper move around McCarter's flailing form. A side kick sent the trooper's subgun flying. The man backpedaled quickly, never seeing Pol's *jo* when it whirred down to tag him out.

McCarter paused, crouched and ready, but he was already out of opponents. Politician, with four unconscious figures at his feet, grinned at him.

Wasting no time on words, Pol led the retreat. McCarter walked backward, keeping an eye on Ironman, who kept

Simms between them and the troops on the other side of the counter.

McCarter's foot scuffed against Ironman's G-11. He scooped it up and rammed it into the sports bag that still hung on Lyons's broad back.

"That asshole you're dragging around is my old CO," McCarter told Lyons as they ducked out the rear door.

"Damn fool talks like a general when he's just muscle on this operation," Lyons muttered.

"You'll hang for this, McCarter," Simms growled.

The rear door didn't provide access to the street. They found themselves on a pier stretching out into the Thames. A police launch idled near the end.

Only the driver remained with the launch. He squinted to try to make out the figures in the dark. By the time he decided to use his searchlight, one of them had already hopped aboard. The skipper found himself an intimate distance from the business end of an H&K caseless.

"The other shore," Politician told him.

"Or what?"

"Or you walk and we try ourselves."

The launch rocked as Simms was pushed on board by Lyons.

"Do what they say," Simms told the skipper. "They're armed and dangerous."

Other forms started to pour out onto the dock from the warehouse. Politician reached in front of the skipper and notched the throttle up, then slapped off the switch for the running lights. At the same time, McCarter threw the painter on board and leaped after it. The skipper frantically slammed the propeller into reverse before the launch rammed the warehouse.

The launch backed up into the Thames. Several SAS troopers dropped into firing position only to break out cursing. It was too dark to tell whether they were aiming at the fugitives or their own men.

"You'll never get out of jail!" Simms shouted over the roar of the motor.

"How's your swimming?" Lyons shouted.

"Bastard's always boasting about it," McCarter bellowed before Simms could say anything.

Lyons heaved on Simms's belt and tossed him overboard.

McCarter laughed. "Now they've got us for polluting the bloody river as well."

The three warriors jumped ashore on the other side of the river. Already sirens could be heard closing in on the area.

"Straight back or we shoot at the waterline!" Politician shouted at the skipper.

The man nodded and gunned away.

McCarter led the way over a ten-foot board wall. Lyons slid his assault rifle back into his sports bag. McCarter was forced to put his in with Politician's.

"What now?" McCarter asked.

"Now you get us out of here to a place where we can lie low," Lyons answered.

McCarter thought for a moment. "Okay, but you pay the ruddy cab fare."

"WE'RE READY FOR THE TRAILER to be removed from the alley," Gadgets reported to Zimmerman.

"Our neighbors will be relieved. The driver's standing by," the manager said as he picked up the telephone.

Gadgets went back to the basement where Lao and Pavlovski were monitoring a row of meters.

"The truck will be moved right away. The tapes still full?"

Lao nodded.

They had a short wait. Gadgets spent some time speculating why they hadn't heard from the rest of the team. Babette shrugged. Lao, with nothing to add, said nothing. Twenty minutes after the truck moved, the recorders whirred softly and two of the meters showed activity.

"Mostly antenna four. Some antenna five," Lao reported.

"Let's see what we have," Gadgets said, leading the way out to the alley.

Whoever had planted the bugs had run a wire out and left six inches of it sticking out as an antenna. The antenna had to receive the signal to activate the dump and then broadcast the reels as they rewound, one at a time. Gadgets was interested in the activating signal. He wanted to know where it originated.

The low-power broadcast unit was a help, strictly line of sight and not more than two miles. Gadgets and Lao rigged up an array of highly directional antennae around the one from the tape recorder. Each antenna was connected to a radio, set to the same frequency as the trigger on the tape recorders. Each circuit included a meter to show the strength of the signal received.

Gadgets sighted down directional antennae four and five. "Probably that office building with the red bricks and stone trim," he announced.

He and the two women shouldered their sports bags and set out.

"What if the phone call comes when we're gone?" Babette asked.

"Isaac can handle it. The important thing is to get a line on the opposition."

When they reached the front of the building, Babette said, "Let me talk to the superintendent first."

In five minutes she was back. "The only new tenants are Electronic Enterprises on the fourth floor."

"A sparkling name. We'll start with them," Gadgets decided.

Gadgets, with one hand inside his sports bag, knocked and tried the door. It was locked and no one responded.

"Watch my back," Gadgets ordered.

In two minutes he was past the ancient tumbler lock. In four more minutes he was out and they were on their way.

When they were out of the building, Gadgets let out his breath with a whoosh.

"I don't know why they're not there by now, but it's the right place. After two confrontations with them, I expect we'll be recognized the next time we show up," Gadgets explained.

"I thought you were itching to meet them," Babette said.

"Not until we can get them all in one place. Quartermaster isn't safe until we break the entire gang."

"Why was no one there?" Lao wondered.

"Someone came and triggered the dump. They must have grabbed their tapes and run the moment they were finished. I suspect it's the office size. The only reason the superintendent rents out that space is that it's too small for a broom closet. There's one battered metal desk, a telephone—I memorized the number—and the recording equipment for the bugs. No room for anything else. Our friends must be listening to the tapes somewhere else."

"But it's line-of-sight?" Lao checked.

Gadgets nodded. "It's line-of-listening, too. I left them two of our bugs."

"Wonder where the rest are," Lao said as they started up the front steps of Quartermaster.

The front door opened. Detective Inspector Quinn stood at the top of the stairs.

"I have a feeling Quinn's about to lay that on us," Gadgets remarked.

9

"Good morning, ladies, Mr. Schwarz. No use coming in. We'll be going straight to the Yard." Owen Quinn's mood was expansive to the point of being jubilant.

A very tired-looking Uriel Isaac appeared behind the detective. Although the night's work and worry about his employees had left dark circles under his eyes, his voice was still crisp and commanding.

"What's the charge, Inspector?"

Lao leaped up the stairs and pushed both men through the front door and shut it.

"The lobby is bugged," Gadgets explained. "Now what are you slamming me in the cooler for this time?"

"David McCarter, Carl Lyons and Rosario Blancanales are charged with murder, assault with a deadly weapon, resisting arrest, unlawful detainment and theft of a launch."

"At least they've been busy. But that doesn't tell us what charges you're going to throw at us," Gadgets reminded him.

"You're accessories."

"Hardly. We didn't know a thing about this until you told us," Gadgets grated.

"I'll have a solicitor at the station to see about this," Isaac snapped. "Where are they being held, Inspector?"

"They're still fugitives."

Gadgets laughed in the man's face. "In other words, they're guilty of living through another terrorist attack. You can't find them, so you're arresting us instead."

Quinn's ears turned scarlet.

Isaac spoke hurriedly, trying to undo the insult in Gadgets's interpretation of the situation. "These three aren't involved. I've been with them throughout most of the night and can swear to that. Nate Zimmerman can testify that he left us here after midnight and returned to find us still working at seven."

"What were you working on?" Quinn asked.

"I don't think we care to go into that at this time," Isaac answered.

"I'm sure you don't. I'm also sure I can hold these three as material witnesses until the time to make the payoff has passed. Do we understand each other?"

Isaac sounded unperturbed by Quinn's guess that they were about to pay off the terrorists. "Perhaps you understand us better than we understand you. May I make a suggestion?"

"I consider myself a reasonable man. I'm listening."

"The ladies and I will go inside. We want to be close to the telephone. You and Mr. Schwarz take a stroll, but you must promise to tell me if you decide to arrest him. I'll need to arrange for a solicitor immediately. Mr. Schwarz, I expect you to give Inspector Quinn a complete briefing regarding our situation. Please make him aware how dangerous it is for police to be seen here."

"I'm not a complete fool," Quinn grumbled. "Why do you think I came alone to collect three armed Yanks? Why do you think I took my own car?"

Isaac smiled. "It seems we've underestimated both your intelligence and your generosity. Will you accept those terms?"

"I'm free to take whatever action I see fit, but did you say you wanted to be notified if I'm going to lock up these three criminals?"

"That's essentially it. Although I'm not sure I'd be happy if you decided to bring policemen onto the premises without my agreement."

Quinn sighed. "I have a feeling this is the only way I'm going to collect straight answers."

He turned and began walking. Gadgets fell into step beside him, sports bag banging on his hip. Isaac, Lao and Babette went inside.

"Isaac made his deal. I haven't made mine," Gadgets began.

"Don't push your luck," Quinn warned him.

"I'm going to fill you in on the situation at Quartermaster. If you want more cooperation, you'll have to tell me more about the charges against my friends. I'm hardly going to risk making their situation worse."

Quinn glanced at Schwarz. The glib patter was gone. He was talking straight and seriously. "Shoot" was all the inspector said.

Gadgets filled the detective in on the situation at Quartermaster—the threats, the bugs, the reference to Megatronics and Gammabase Delta. He described what had actually happened at the airport, including the stashing of two weapons. Gadgets stressed how seriously they took the threats. He told Quinn about finding the terrorists' office but failed to mention the small case of illegal entry in order to plant his bugs. Gadgets admitted that the other half of the team was trying to trace the terrorists through their weapons.

When he was finished talking, they walked two blocks before the detective spoke. "Your friends went too far. They stormed into a warehouse that channels weapons to the IRA. There was a shoot-out that made World War II look tame. It took twelve minutes for the Flying Squad and SAS Lightning Response Team to move in. By that time the place was littered with bodies. Then your friends kidnapped an SAS officer and forced the skipper of a police launch to take them across the river. The SAS officer is pressing every charge in the book. They can't get out of this one."

It was Gadgets's turn to think before he spoke. Half a block later he said, "You owe us the rest of the story."

"There is no more, except that if you hear from your friends you'd better advise them to give themselves up."

"Tell us about the guns Scotland Yard sold to the terrorists."

Quinn started. "That's a serious charge."

"So is murder, kidnapping and the other things you're trumping up against us."

Quinn changed the subject. "So now you're waiting for the extortionists to give you delivery instructions. And you're going to pay off. There's no excuse for not notifying the Yard. We may not like it, but we cooperate in these matters."

Gadgets switched the conversation right back to his point of attack. "When we establish that the Yard knew about the terrorists and even supplied them with weapons, no jury is going to believe we should have cooperated with the Yard."

Quinn kept himself under better control the second time the accusation was made. His voice was quiet when he said, "That's the second time you've made that statement. Can you substantiate it?"

"No, but it can be substantiated with a small amount of investigation."

"No proof. What's your theory?"

"Britain has an admirable record for keeping its weapons out of the wrong hands. My own country, unfortunately, has sold so many weapons without questioning the buyer that American weapons are a glut on both the legal and illegal markets.

"Helen's Tea Company funnels arms to the IRA. The U.S. is the major source of IRA weapons, supplying so many that the IRA sometimes sells surplus arms to other terrorists and to criminals. So the terrorists we're after buy British-made weapons from Helen's. My friends go there to ask why and both the Flying Squad and SAS are there in twelve minutes. The place was staked out."

Gadgets turned them back toward Quartermaster before continuing. "How did CID learn about Helen's? I'm willing to bet they found it by selling a batch of Brit-made weapons, then traced the flow. The sale had to be large enough that only the main IRA supply line could handle it. The IRA wasn't sure about the shipment, so they passed it on to the terrorist group we're after."

Quinn opened his mouth to speak, but Gadgets finished quickly before he could be interrupted. "When my friends are arrested, have you thought about the press coverage? They're being accused of not cooperating with the police who supplied the terrorist weapons."

"You play hardball."

"I nail my wickets together, too."

"You realize the publicity could be suppressed in the national interest?"

Gadgets shook his head. "You wouldn't have a chance. Too many questions would be asked from the States."

"Who are you? And don't give me another dose of those 'simple businessman' salts."

"Stalemate?"

Quinn rubbed a long hand over his bristly jaw. "No. A very self-righteous officer of the SAS is demanding blood. He seems to take it personally that he was kidnapped, then thrown into the Thames to swim home. He has enough pull to get his blood, too."

"So?"

"I'll have to take you in until your friends are caught. Then we'll see whether or not to charge you with complicity."

"And you'll assume personal responsibility for the lives of the Quartermaster employees?"

Quinn snorted. "I suppose you're assuming that responsibility."

"It's one of the things they pay us for."

"This is England, not the Wild West. You can't go around shooting up people. And you can't go around carrying weapons."

"Why? If Scotland Yard supplies the terrorists, at least they shouldn't object to us supplying ourselves."

"Your group messed up months of investigative work. You realize that?"

"I don't give a damn how much work anyone did. Tell me about the results."

Quinn flushed and walked for another half block before saying, "Some people will call this blackmail."

"I'd call it survival. We're not the ones who screwed up."

"You're still going to find that most of this is blamed on your group. What do you expect me to do about it?"

"You know that none of the three of us was involved in the fiasco at the tea company. Taking us in is simple harassment."

Quinn walked in silence until they reached Quartermaster once more. Suddenly he said, "Selling those weapons was Simms's idea. It's not something Scotland Yard was happy about, but he got Home Office to go along."

"Not Major Geoffrey Simms?"

"Right. You know him?"

"Only of him. McCarter turned up once claiming Simms had broken into his apartment and tried to kill him. Those two love each other about as much as cats love dogs. Simms is lucky to be alive if McCarter was near him."

"Is that so? Major Simms made no mention of the background." Quinn stroked his large unshaven jaw. Then he straightened his tired shoulders, as if he'd come to a decision after a long struggle.

"I'll have to initiate the manhunt for your friends. Keep in touch."

With that he strode off.

Gadgets entered the building and suggested that Babette and Lao accompany him on another walk around the block.

"IT'S NEARLY NOON. I'd have expected our friends to call before this," Isaac said in a soft voice.

Isaac, Schwarz, Lao Ti and Pavlovski had been camped in the chairman's office since they'd returned from their walk and planning session. Gadgets and Lao were stretched out on the carpet, grabbing sleep whenever and wherever they could. Babette and Isaac were sipping tea.

Babette gestured to the telephone and shook her head. She knew no call would come through. Lyons wouldn't know who was listening in.

"I was thinking about the delivery instructions. They said today."

"Everything ready?"

"Yes."

Three minutes later the telephone rang.

Gadgets rolled to his feet and put on a single earphone, allowing him to listen to whatever was said in the office rented by the terrorists.

Isaac scooped up the handset, saying, "Isaac here."

"And how many others?" a voice asked. It wasn't the rasping voice that had threatened him three days ago. The new voice was definitely a man's.

Isaac raised an eyebrow at Gadgets, who nodded and held up three fingers, indicating that the phone call was being made from the rented office and that Isaac should answer honestly.

"I have three members of our security firm with me. They've been instructed to make the delivery."

"You'll make the delivery," the voice said.

"I hardly think so. You chaps tried to kidnap me once. If I made the delivery, you'd have me. I'll pay to protect my employees, but I won't pay that much." Isaac delivered the prepared argument with a carefully controlled voice. It made him sound genuinely frightened.

After a four-second pause, the voice asked, "Are you ready to take down delivery instructions?"

"Of course."

Whoever was on the other end of the wire was annoyed at the mild rebuke. He rattled off the instructions quickly.

"Your man is to take the 1:14 to Eastbourne. When the train pulls in, he has six minutes to catch the 197 Berlina bus. He's to get a seat up top on the left-hand side. When the bus goes past the Parade gardens, he will throw the package into the flowers at the fourth streetlight. He will then stay on the bus until it returns him to the station. Do you have that?"

"Yes."

"Then do it."

Isaac replaced the handset slowly and watched as Gadgets continued to monitor the conversation in the terrorists' office.

Three minutes later, Gadgets looked up and nodded at the door. Then he set the bug to record anything else that was said if the terrorists returned to their hole in the wall.

The meeting adjourned to the boardroom. Gadgets swept it again before he'd allow anyone to start speaking. Lao picked up Babette's war bag and disappeared.

"Still clean," he reported. "Is the payoff ready?"

Isaac nodded. "Bank messenger brought it yesterday. I wrapped the money and disks in a brown paper package. You'll deliver it?"

Gadgets shook his head. "Babette will. I have the job of rounding up the reserve team."

Isaac was surprised at the answer but said nothing.

"I need a way for four people to beat the package to Eastbourne by a half hour and I need another package just like the one you made up to hold the money and disks."

"You're not thinking of fouling the delivery?" Isaac sounded worried.

"On the contrary. I'm trying to guarantee it."

Isaac left the boardroom and returned with a padded envelope, the type used for sending bulky, fragile items through the mail. He produced a matching envelope and a stapler from the mail room. He handed them over without protest but moved reluctantly.

"I'll try to arrange for the helicopter from a client company. They have their own helipad near East India Dock

Road. Otherwise, I doubt we'll find a hire firm in time. We'll be forced to drive.''

Gadgets was only half listening. He was flipping through a telephone book.

"That in the same direction as this?" Gadgets demanded, his finger pointing out an address.

"No. It's in the opposite direction."

"Then have the helicopter land at that address."

"How do you know there's suitable space?"

"A chopper's made a pickup there before. When we're sure our tail's clean, we'll stop at a pay phone so you can order the chopper."

Gadgets jammed newspaper and a small transmitter into the second padded envelope and stapled it shut. He handed the dummy envelope to Babette. She took it and left the boardroom, her pink running shoes squeaking on the polished floor.

"You said there'd be no funny business," Isaac objected.

"There won't be on our side, but I suspect the other side has some tricks up its sleeve. At the right time the right package will get tossed."

"I said I'd go along, but this is beginning to look like a double play."

Gadgets laughed. "More like a double, double play. Let's move." He led the way out the door, stuffing the payoff package into his sports bag.

Gadgets swept the Bentley twice and looked under it, under the hood and in the compartment the chauffeur insisted on calling the boot. Only then did he climb in so that they could get under way.

"As soon as you're positive we're not followed, go to the Kowloon Restaurant in Soho," he told the driver.

Seventeen minutes later they were in front of the unpretentious restaurant that catered to a predominantly Chinese clientele.

"There's a telephone," Gadgets told Isaac.

Giving the American a quizzical look, the industrialist climbed out to make his call. Gadgets wound down his window and watched the crowd, seventy percent Oriental, flow past the car.

A small boy moved past, carrying a large bundle of linen tied with twine. Gadgets threw him the padded envelope containing the disks and the money. He shuffled along with the crowd and disappeared around the corner.

When Isaac climbed back into the car, he failed to notice that Gadgets no longer held the package.

"It's all laid on," he told Gadgets, "but they're as curious as I am as to why we're going to a school for butlers and valets."

"To attend a self-defense class," Gadgets answered.

Isaac rolled his eyes and refused to ask the mad American any more questions.

LAO HAD NO TROUBLE catching a taxi to the Chinese section of the city.

She needed boy's clothing, used boy's clothing. She also needed some sort of package to hide the weapons she carried.

Having been brought up in the martial arts since the age of three, it never occurred to her to waste time looking for appropriate stores. Instead, she chose to search the extensive Chinese section for a traditional martial arts hall.

Although she was a mixture of Vietnamese and Mongolian, brought up in Japan, she knew she could get cooperation from Chinese martial artists. It was one community that usually managed to transcend national boundaries.

Once she found other martial artists, it took her little time to acquire boy's clothing and a bundle for her weapons. When she emerged from the locker room, two large Chinese black belts grabbed her arms while another snatched the bundle away.

Lao threw her feet back and tucked into a ball, as if she were going to do a forward somersault. When her feet were over her head, they straightened like pistons, kicking her two captors on the side of the head. They staggered apart but refused to let go.

Lao's feet swung back while her captors grinned. But just before she was upright once more, the feet spread to catch each man behind the inside knee. They leaned in, fighting to keep their footing. Lao lunged forward and dragged them with her.

The martial artist on her right lost his balance. As he stumbled in front of her, Lao's foot shot out, catching him in the solar plexus. He let go of her arm and concentrated on breathing.

The man who'd snatched her bundle tossed it aside and launched himself in a flying kick aimed at her chest.

Lao didn't try to spin away from the flying kick. Instead, she let her knees stay loose, allowing the kick to pass over her head. On the way down she slammed her free fist into the groin of the black belt who was still holding her arm, trying to turn his hold into a throw.

The recipient of the punch loosened his grip. She pulled her arm loose and whirled to take care of the martial artist who thought leaping in the air was good technique.

He'd landed on his feet and was spinning to renew the attack. Lao kicked his thigh to increase his rate of spin. When his back was to her, she planted a fist in his kidneys that made his knees buckle but didn't do permanent damage.

She bowed to the master of the training hall. He returned the bow and barked something at his students. They forgot their suffering long enough to struggle to their feet and bow to Lao. As they were lowering their faces, their disgusted teacher gave them each a rap on the back of the neck, sending all three crashing to the floor again.

Lao's credentials had been established. She had shown her competency, not so much in the success of her resistance as in her ability to resist strongly without doing permanent damage to the attackers. Having shown an exceptional proficiency, she was escorted from the practice hall and her money was refused.

The small computer whiz reached the assigned corner in Soho just after Isaac stepped into the telephone booth. She accepted the package from Gadgets and deposited it in her bundle. When she was around the corner, she hailed a taxi and told him to rush to Waterloo Station.

THE BENTLEY STOPPED in front of an Edwardian building with a discreet plaque on the door, announcing the Neville Academy of Butler and Valet Instruction.

As they got out of the car, Isaac asked, "Where's the envelope?"

"On its way."

"What are you trying to have off, Mr. Schwarz?"

"You're committed, Isaac. We play this my way."

Uriel Isaac shrugged and followed Gadgets to the door. His lips were set in a grim line.

"Stay out of the way when the rhubarb starts cooking," Gadgets said. "And hold this." He handed the short industrialist his war bag as if he were handing golf clubs to a caddy.

One butler opened the door while two more stood at attention and observed.

"Yes?"

Gadgets slouched in the doorway.

"Mr. McCarter, please."

"I'm sorry. There's no one here by that name."

Gadgets's slouch turned into a leap. His shoulder caught the surprised butler in the gut, driving him back into his two observers. All three rolled out of the way like trained athletes and came up in fighting crouches. One of them let out a shrill, unbutlerlike whistle. A number of men in dark suits appeared in the plush hallway, while others tore down the ornate staircase two steps at a time.

"My God!" Isaac breathed. "What's he got us into?"

10

Gadgets grabbed the first of the reinforcements and used him to bowl over another. He spun away from a kick and under a karate punch. The Able Team warrior used a short jab to the armpit of a gentleman's gentleman and quickly disabled him.

Gadgets adopted a deep squat, facing the antagonists who were spreading out and trying to surround him. A shrill whistle froze the group.

McCarter's voice barked from the stairs, "Back off before he starts to play rough. There's a time to fight and a time to run. You blokes should have seen that he wasn't worried about facing a dozen of you and asked yourselves why."

"Just a minute—" Gadgets began. He hadn't been worried about taking on McCarter's self-defense class because he knew McCarter couldn't resist coming out of hiding to see how his students were doing. It had only been a matter of time until McCarter recognized him.

Gadgets was cut off by a squat, ruggedly built butler-in-training who protested, "We would of 'ad 'im off 'is feet in no time."

McCarter's smile barely hid a veiled threat.

"Kindly oblige my student by taking this lying down," he told Gadgets.

Politician and Ironman appeared behind McCarter, with their war bags ready to go.

"No time. The payoff's going down," Gadgets answered.

"If you're in a rush, don't waste time arguing," McCarter answered.

Uriel Isaac decided it was safe to step inside and close the door. He still held Gadgets's weapons bag.

Schwarz sighed and lay on his back in the hall under the ornate crystal chandelier.

"Okay, Hastings," McCarter told the protesting student. "Choose five of your friends and show me what you'd do when you took him off his feet."

"It wouldn't mean much," Hastings protested. "We'd 'ave to 'old back from your friend."

"Don't hold anything back. Give it your best go or fail the class."

With that threat to motivate him, Hastings chose five fit-looking men. They moved in two directions to surround Gadgets, then they all moved in at once. Two flew back as Gadgets's feet snapped into their thighs. Normally he would have aimed for and broken their knees.

Two managed to fall on Gadgets's chest, scrambling to pin his arms. Hastings reserved the pleasure of slamming his fist down at Gadgets's face. The fist never connected. Gadgets's right foot flashed back from its kick and massaged Hastings's face on the return trip. He was knocked on his ass before his punch connected.

The force of the return kick brought Gadgets's hips clear of the polished floor. He continued back until he was standing on his neck and shoulder tops, his left leg reaching for the floor behind. The two students pinning his arms held on as if their lives depended on it. But Gadgets's left leg suddenly bent, closing around the neck of one of his captors. Gadgets straightened his back, breaking the hold the man to his left had on him.

The freed left hand smashed into the nerve junction under the triceps of the other captor. That student's right arm released its grip as he howled in pain.

The two who had been kicked away closed in from the sides.

Gadgets rolled onto his stomach. During the roll, his top leg lashed out, catching one man on the forehead, knocking him back to crash into the wall. Then Gadgets was on his hands and knees. He mule-kicked back and up, sending someone else staggering.

Instead of getting to his feet, Gadgets seemed to stumble. He rolled, spun on his hip and grabbed Hastings's ankles, dumping him on his ass once again.

"Enough," McCarter roared.

The students backed off. Gadgets rolled easily to his feet. Immediately two of the students tackled him with whisks, brushing every bit of lint off his suit.

As they brushed, McCarter said, "You've just had the privilege of seeing one of the few masters of both Monkey and Drunken-Style kung fu. Get it through your thick skulls that you take nothing for granted. Just because a man is on his back doesn't mean he's going to be peaceful. It doesn't even mean he isn't going to shoot you!"

With that, McCarter led Able Team out of the Neville School. The throb of a helicopter sounded directly overhead.

"Some service," McCarter admitted. "How did you find us?"

Gadgets found them because he had remembered McCarter once talking about the frustrations of teaching gentlemen's gentlemen that the Marquis of Queensberry had nothing to say about survival.

"Just asked about until someone could tell me where to find the worst self-defense class in London," Gadgets replied.

Surprisingly McCarter wasn't upset. He threw back his head and roared with laughter.

"I swear," he told the group, "if someone starts shooting at one of those idiots, my student's going to stand still to give the bullets a sporting chance."

"They that way when they graduate?" Lyons asked.

McCarter laughed again. "Hell, no!"

By the time the conversation was finished, they were shouting against the noise of the landing helicopter, a commercial chopper similar to the Westland Wessex. The military version of the same helicopter was the Royal Navy's choice for antisubmarine and rescue work.

The warriors quickly buckled into the passenger seats while Isaac gave instructions to the pilot and copilot. Then he came back and buckled in. It was his war; no one suggested he should stay behind.

"GENTLEMEN, our profit margin has risen for the forty-eighth consecutive year. I feel it safe to predict that the Baked Bean will take over the home computer market."

The speaker wore a gray suit with a vest that buttoned to within four inches of his chin, and a permanent sneer registering his disapproval of practically everything. It was the sneer, of course, that denoted his high position among the Bostonian aristocracy.

Around the boardroom table of the Paul Revere Accounting Machine Company of Boston sat five other gentlemen whose conservative suits made standard bankers' wear look like plaid horse blankets by comparison. The youngest of the directors would be seventy in a month's time.

James Jason FitzHugh IV continued his report to the board. "I am pleased that our marketing strategy is proving to be most successful. We have heavily advertised the Baked Bean as a business and educational computer. At the same time we have included as standard equipment two joysticks and two mice. The software community has responded with a large number of mindless games.

"The results, I'm pleased to announce, are that an unprecedented number of households have bought this computer to help their offspring with their education and to use for household applications. I understand someone will be bringing out a word processor for the Baked Bean some-time next year. That should considerably enhance our serious computer image.

"Furthermore—"

James Jason FitzHugh IV was rudely interrupted when the door to the boardroom was knocked off its hinges. The person who stepped inside and stood, marring the mahogany door with her combat boots, did not seem to be the right type for a Bostonian boardroom.

She was five foot nine, broad-shouldered and wide. She had a crooked nose and a gap-toothed grin. Her greasy hair was tied in a wad on the top of her head. The gray rag that tied the hair might have been white once. Her fists hung at her sides, looking more like deformed clubs than hands. When she spoke, her voice rasped like a file over thin metal.

"Where the hell is the Cray?"

"I beg your pardon? This is a private meeting," Fitz-Hugh told the intruder.

While the speaker confronted the woman, another of the elderly directors opened his briefcase telephone and punched out the police emergency number.

Jishin was used to inspiring fear among men. Here she found not fear but indignation that someone should act out of place. She preferred fear; it kept reactions predictable. She strode farther into the room, determined to make an example of the pompous ass who remained standing at the head of the table.

She didn't count on the oldest member of the board. A ninety-year-old swung his cane, hooked Jishin's ankle and yanked her off her feet. She rolled and came to her feet, swearing.

Jishin saw a director at the other end of the table with a telephone in his hand. Her terrorists had cut telephone lines before starting the raid, and she was seething at the indignity of being tripped as if she were a novice. She didn't think to concentrate her attack on the man with the telephone.

The director with the cane was the first to receive the full brunt of the terrorist's wrath. Jishin snatched the cane from his hand and swung the offending crook down on his frail skull, easily cracking it.

James Jason FitzHugh didn't believe Jishin was showing proper respect for her elders. He pushed back the antique ladder-back chair that sat behind him and charged. Her leg came up, bent at the knee, then straightened with a snap. Jishin's combat boot smashed through two chair rungs and into the bottom of the chair seat. FitzHugh was propelled back across the room to smash into the wall and slide down to the floor.

The director at the end of the table returned the telephone handset and closed his briefcase. Only then did Jishin realize the police had really been notified. The two other old men shuffled around to stand on either side of the man who had telephoned. The three stood side by side, confident of the righteousness of their cause.

Jishin put both hands on the other end of the ten-foot-long table, hunched her shoulders and drove with her legs. The two-hundred-pound antique slid across the polished floor. The three defiant directors had hips crushed as if they'd been struck by a truck. One died instantly; the other two screamed in agony for some minutes before succumbing to internal bleeding.

From outside the room came the screams of employees and the occasional rattle of automatic weapons.

Jishin moved to FitzHugh and shook him.

"Where is the Cray computer?"

"For pity's sake, woman! We sold it a month ago."

Jishin showed her disgust by pistol-whipping FitzHugh until he lost consciousness and eventually died. Then she went out to round up her troops. She could already hear the sound of sirens.

"Save the rest for hostages," she bellowed.

EDWARD ZAPPA, known affectionately as "Zap" to his subordinates, was a twenty-five-year veteran of the Boston Police Department. He was especially proud of his new posting, commanding a Threat Response Team. It had taken his team exactly thirteen minutes to reach the Paul Revere Accounting Machine Company from the time of the telephone call reporting machine gun fire.

The Paul Revere Accounting Machine Company, known as PRAM to everyone except its directors, was located in the southeast portion of Boston on Route 93. The three-story warehouse and office building had an elaborate limestone-and-glass front and cinder-block construction on the other three sides.

The Threat Response Team rolled into the parking lot to find men brandishing automatic weapons and loading hostages into private cars. Terrified workers were being forced into the driver's seats of their own cars. Three or four fatigue-clad men rode in each vehicle, keeping their weapons trained on the hapless driver.

A hail of automatic weapon fire stopped the police vehicles before they could plug the parking lot.

A hoarse-voiced woman yelled, "Any interference and we blow up the building and everyone in it."

Before the police could assimilate the threat, the cars roared out of the parking lot, weaving in the hands of terrified drivers. A hail of gunfire forced the police to earth. No one returned fire. It would be impossible to kill three or four terrorists without killing a hostage.

The moment the last car and hostage left the parking lot, Zap was on the radio demanding air cover to trace the escape cars. He signaled an unmarked car to try to keep the deadly cavalcade in sight.

By the time he was through, some of the veteran officers were staggering from the building, looking white.

"Wish the bastards had blown up the building," one told Zappa. "No one alive. Some of them didn't go easy."

The car dispatched to follow the terrorists returned with a woman in the passenger seat. She was bleeding from the forehead and gave no sign of knowing where she was.

"They threw this one on the road in front of me. I had no time to stop," the officer reported. He was shaking from having hit the woman and from the rage he felt at the inhumanity of the criminals.

Zappa returned to his radio to order one ambulance, a couple of forensic crews and a convoy of meat wagons. A hot rage was beginning to consume his gut. He needed federal help on this one. He'd phone the Justice Department the minute he got back to his office.

BABETTE PAVLOVSKI EMERGED from the railway station into Eastbourne's confusing streets. She blinked against the glare of the sun from the white-painted buildings. Most of the roads were one way. Clutching the brown parcel, she strode into the sun, trying to find the place where she was to catch the Berlina bus.

She became aware of several people who seemed to be aimlessly wandering wherever she went in search of the bus stop. An Oriental boy with a bundle of laundry meandered ahead of her. Two men walked on the other side of the road. At each intersection they chose their direction only after she committed herself. She'd pass pairs of men on some corners, and one of them would start to saunter in her direction. She was beginning to feel she was in a parade.

She arrived at the correct bus stop with two minutes to spare. A long queue of patient Englishmen stood along the curb. The Oriental boy was already in line. Two of six men who had walked from the station lined up between herself and the Oriental boy, who waited patiently, never looking back at her. Three more men drifted in to stand behind Babette.

The double-decker bus pulled to the curb, and the line moved quickly. Another man came and stood, apparently waiting for the line to pass. Babette noticed the Slavic planes of his face. The Oriental boarded, then the next two passengers. Just as she was about to board the bus, hands seized her from behind, and the man at the side of the bus grabbed the parcel she carried.

"Do not move. Do not shout. Or we kill," an accented voice spoke in her ear.

She was pulled to one side, and one man smiled and waved the bus on. The terrorists gave Babette a quick pat-down to make sure she was unarmed.

"No weapons. You live," someone muttered.

The man with the package was already strolling down the sidewalk, a hundred yards away. Those who held her suddenly let go, turned and walked off. The entire operation was done with such precision that no one else had noticed. If anyone had seen the tall graceful woman taken from the line waiting for the bus, it appeared she was merely among friends. The terrorists' bodies had blocked people passing by from seeing the frisk.

When they withdrew as quickly as they had gathered, Babette was left standing on the sidewalk, looking for a friendly face, wondering what to do next.

11

Eugene Shaughnesy was bored. Driving a hack in a quiet place like Eastbourne might be good for the ulcer, but he was sure the boredom would be just as fatal. He had decided it was also just as painful. He was sitting at the airport between Worthing and Eastbourne, waiting for a company helicopter to touch down at the corner of the field. Some big shot had booked the taxi before leaving London. He had specified room for five.

Businessmen were a bore. They tipped ten percent and expected twenty percent's service. Shaughnesy yawned as the big Westland settled to the ground. He climbed out of the limousine, knowing the men would expect him to carry their briefcases.

The fifty-six-foot rotors hadn't started to slow before the passengers came spilling out. Four big men carried athletes' bags labeled Almost Celtics. They didn't move like athletes; they moved like hunting cats. In the midst of them walked one short man without a bag, looking as if he were enjoying himself.

One man, with brown hair, carried two bags. Shaughnesy reached for one of them, only to have his hand pushed away. He stood beside the door to the limousine, deciding how best to state his protest. By the time he decided what to say, everyone was in the car.

A big blond guy with cold eyes got back out and asked, "What are you waiting for?"

Shaughnesy took one look at the man and edited his complaint down to, "Right away, sir."

"The train station. Rush," the blonde said.

"No rush, guv'nor. No train leaving for two hours."

"We're not leaving. We're meeting one. Go."

Eugene Shaughnesy went.

The meanest of the crew jumped out at the railroad station, but they didn't go in. Instead they split up and headed in different directions. Shaughnesy couldn't figure it out, but he had no inclination to ask questions. He turned to the two in the back seat, the small one and a big one with white hair.

The big one said, "The seaside gardens. We feel like a stroll."

"Ah, these other gentlemen..." Shaughnesy began as he put the limo in gear.

"What other gentlemen?" the big one asked.

The driver decided he didn't really want to know.

THE THREE WARRIORS at the train station faded into doorways, staying well back to cut down the odds of being spotted. Lyons and Gadgets had their communicators. McCarter had to work visually and by instinct. Gadgets had the inconvenience of carrying two war bags—Babette's and his own.

When the procession to the bus stop began, the trio from Stony Man followed it. They watched Babette being cleverly neutralized while her package walked away. McCarter moved off, keeping the package in sight. Lyons followed the men who'd held Pavlovski while the package was taken. Gadgets waited until he was sure Babette was no longer watched, then approached and handed her the sports bag containing the G-11 and Steyr.

"Am I glad to see you!" Babette exclaimed. "What now?"

"Now we teach your recent acquaintances that snatching parcels is frowned on. Besides, it isn't polite."

"Good. I hate being mauled."

Gadgets clicked his communicator three times, then once to attract Ironman's attention.

"Yeah?"

"Where are you?"

"Block north, then east. They're beginning to flock."

"Where's McCarter?"

"He seems to be the reason they're flocking."

Gadgets broke into a run, Babette at his heels. They didn't overtake the others for two more blocks. By the time they arrived on the scene, four terrorists had converged on McCarter. Lyons had been marked and circled by another four. There was no sign of the thug with the package.

Lyons and McCarter burst into action in the same second, as if they had heard the same bell to start the round. McCarter let loose a flurry of tae kwon do kicks that flattened two of the terrorists before they could leap back. The other two decided hand-to-hand combat wasn't as good an idea as it had first seemed. They backpedaled furiously, reaching for their automatics.

Lyons stood with a quizzical look on his face, as if he didn't have the remotest idea why four strange men should approach him from four directions. He stood loosely, his knees slightly bent, his hands at his sides. It was a reaction that none of the four attackers expected. They exchanged puzzled glances.

The momentary hesitation while the terrorists established eye contact was what Lyons had been waiting for. His left elbow jerked back to bury itself in a solar plexus. His right foot taught a knee to bend backward. The two on each side of Lyons pulled knives from forearm sheaths and lunged toward him.

Lyons's left arm pumped forward again. His fist, with the center knuckle extended, smashed into a knife hand. The knuckle buried itself at the point where the bones of the thumb meet the bones from the first finger. The hand loosened its grip, and the knife dropped.

Lyons's right hand closed on the wrist of the other knife wielder. The terrorist smashed home a left hook that made Ironman's knees wobble, but he merely tightened his grip on the wrist.

The terrorist brought back his fist for another punch, only to find his fist seized in an iron grip. He glanced back to find a smiling brown-haired gentleman holding on to the closed fist. As Gadgets squeezed, bones began to crack.

The disarmed terrorist made the mistake of grabbing his knife in his left hand and charging Lyons once more. His knife was held to the side and ready to slice Lyons's leg when he tried to kick.

Lyons lunged forward on his left leg in the style of a fencer, then he whipped his right leg through into a thrust kick. His stride was so long and rapid that he dragged the other knife wielder and Gadgets along.

The long stride and thrust kick brought him up to the attacker a split second before he was ready for combat. Lyons's foot smashed through the slashing knife and into the base of the man's sternum. The force of the kick lifted the terrorist two inches off the ground. Then he collapsed, unable to remember how to breathe.

The two gunmen separated from McCarter in opposite directions. McCarter had few choices. Going for his weapon would catch him in a cross fire. Not only were his own odds for survival poor, but innocent people were bound to be hit.

The sidewalks were busy and people had stopped to look. The fights had begun so quickly that only a handful of people realized something was wrong.

McCarter was forced to ignore one gunman and close with the other. Three long strides brought him up to the terrorist just as a Webley cleared leather. McCarter's long arm drove forward. The heel of his hand connected with the side of the gun barrel, driving it into the terrorist's collarbone. The clavicle broke with an audible snap.

The fighting Englishman took another step, driving his other fist into the terrorist's gut. The Bulgarian's breath exploded from his lungs.

The other terrorist steadied his right wrist with his left hand and lined up a perfect head shot at ten feet. McCarter's brown hair was the only thing he saw over the sights.

The terrorist definitely didn't see the tall thin woman who dived through the crowd and tackled him from the side. She hit him the way a shark hits a barracuda. His shot went wide, just over the head of an onlooker.

The crowd decided they'd seen enough gunfighting from ringside and began a panicked retreat.

The terrorist being stretched between Lyons and Gadgets screamed as his arms were pulled from their sockets.

"Where's the parcel going? Who's in charge?" Lyons barked.

The man who was trying to blow McCarter's head off went down under Babette's weight, but he twisted and brought the barrel slamming across her forehead. She fell away, temporarily stunned.

The terrorist found himself sitting on the sidewalk presented with two targets—Babette on her hands and knees, shaking her head to clear it, and McCarter who was finishing his man off with a double-handed punch to the back of the neck.

The gunman was bringing his sights to bear on McCarter once more when the terrorist racked between Lyons and Schwarz screamed, "No more. I talk."

Without hesitation the seated terrorist lined up on his comrade and squeezed the trigger. Three 224-grain .455s changed the screams of cooperation into gurgles of death.

He swung the notch-and-bar sight to Ironman, the next closest target. But before he could squeeze the trigger, Babette's foot lashed out from where she knelt on the sidewalk. Her instep caught him across the throat and knocked him back, cursing and choking. The reaction squeezed off two more bullets that just missed Lyons.

McCarter took two running steps and a jump. His instep came down across the terrorist's throat, rendering him permanently peaceful.

Lyons and Gadgets dropped their dead prisoner.

"This is the time when I usually run like bloody hell," McCarter said calmly.

Lyons turned to Gadgets. "Which way?"

Gadgets pulled a small receiver from a clip on his belt and played with a directional antenna on top of it.

"Tallyho," he said, pointing to the left.

The three men and Babette took off running. The terrorists were out of commission, and no one else seemed inclined to chase them.

At the next corner they paused long enough to let the electronics wizard make another reading. He pointed, and they began another sprint. Ahead of them the lone terrorist with the parcel was getting into a taxi.

It took less than a minute to hail another cab. Gadgets sat beside the driver and gave directions, leaving the other three to squeeze into the back.

"Wot's that?" the driver asked, referring to the directional finder in Gadgets's hands.

"Carbon monoxide indicator. We're trying to find where it's thinnest. This thing makes a hell of a racket in the absence of poisonous gases."

"Shouldn't that be the other way round, guv'nor? Making noise when it detects poison stuff?"

Gadgets looked shocked. "In jolly old England, man? You'd go deaf."

After they'd been traveling five minutes, the driver started to laugh. "Fat lot o' good that fancy machine is. It's taking us down to the shore. Any fool knows there's less fumes down there."

"The waterfront gardens?" Ironman asked from the back seat.

"That's where we're headed, guv'nor."

"Then step on it!" Lyons snapped.

ROSARIO BLANCANALES and Uriel Isaac beat the bus to the Parade Gardens near the pier. They had the taxi drop them a block past and walked back, anxiously scanning for a way to watch without being seen. They squinted against the sun, although the air was cold and damp.

An elderly man of hefty build shuffled along the broad sidewalk. He wore a filthy coat and cloth cap. The bulge in his coat pocket looked suspiciously like a bottle. Politician stopped short.

"How would you like fifty pounds?" he asked the old-timer.

The man squinted at him with watery eyes.

"Ain't fit to kill anyone these days. Wot you have in mind?"

"Fifty for your cap, coat and bottle, right now."

"You lost your bloomin' coconut?"

Politician answered by pulling out his roll and counting off five ten-pound notes.

The old man looked across the street where a new coat would cost him only thirty pounds. He snatched the money first, dumped the coat and cap on the sidewalk and walked off as quickly as he could.

"Get a table in that restaurant," Pol told Isaac, pointing with his *jo* as he picked up the coat with the other hand. "Sit where you can see out, but don't sit in the window. We don't want you recognized."

Isaac nodded and walked briskly along the street. When he was seated inside the restaurant, he looked through the window. The old man had taken his coat back!

A second look told him that it was really Rosario Blancanales in the greasy coat and worn cap. But the old man's walk was being duplicated exactly. The warrior shuffled to a park bench in the middle of the gardens as if he wasn't sure his legs would last until he got there. One hand, almost out of sight in the long sleeve, kept patting the pocket holding the bottle. The reassurance of the bottle seemed to work; he made it to the bench and collapsed gratefully. His chin fell to his chest, and he suddenly became part of the scenery.

LAO TI HAD KEPT a protective eye on Babette throughout the train trip. She'd left the train quickly and walked ahead to the bus stop. It took an act of will to board the bus while Pavlovski was being detained, but covering the gymnast was the responsibility of the rest of the team. Lao's job was to make sure the package was delivered to the pickup spot.

The terrorists might plan to hijack the package early, but Lao's job was to prevent that. The terrorists couldn't be allowed to claim that the delivery wasn't made as specified. If they had something else planned, that was their tough luck.

Lao fought her way up the winding steps and found a seat on the left side of the bus. She put her bundle between herself and the window and occupied the aisle seat, unwilling to risk a tug of war over the package. It contained the money and software, her clothes and her weapons.

Lao carefully surveyed the other passengers on the upper deck. The November chill helped; most stayed below. No one sat close enough to give her trouble without warning.

When she caught sight of the gardens, she drew the padded envelope out of her bundle. Even in November the gardens were a blaze of color. Low bushy plants with scarlet-and-maroon foliage seemed to burn in the sunlight. Small yellow and gold flowers appeared in clumps. The carefully tended grass was a dark but lush green. Beyond the carefully laid-out gardens, the occasional whitecap sparkled on the dull gray of the rolling sea.

As the bus reached the center of the stretch of gardens, Lao heaved the envelope into a bed of yellow flowers planted in a star shape and surrounded by a circle of deep green foliage.

She immediately put her head down in case of sniper fire, but none came. She waited calmly until the bus was out of sight of the gardens. Then she hastened down the steps and off the bus. She walked back toward the gardens slowly, as if she was in no hurry to be anywhere in particular. The leisurely pace seemed to be the norm for Eastbourne.

WHEN THE PACKAGE LANDED in the flower garden, a thick-set Japanese man in a conservative business suit went over to investigate. From his place on the park bench, Politician watched without moving his head.

The stocky Japanese was considering how best to retrieve the parcel without trampling the flowers when he was hailed by someone from a taxi. He paused to watch the person struggle with the currency and pay the driver. When the newcomer approached, he was carrying a package identical to the one in the flower bed.

The Japanese wrinkled his forehead and snatched the parcel from the newcomer. He ripped it open and pulled out scrap paper. A small bundle of wires and electronic parts fell at his feet. He picked it up, looked at it, cursed and threw it toward the ocean.

The newcomer lacked the delicacy of his superior. He waded into the flower bed and picked up the other parcel. As he stepped back onto the sidewalk, a whizzing stick cracked against his wrist, causing him to drop the package.

He looked up to discover that the old man on the bench had moved with remarkable speed to prevent him from taking the package. Before he could react, two more things happened to further confuse the situation:

A voice exclaimed, "Hoy! What's happening here?"

A taxi stopped. Four men climbed out, looking worse for wear. They vaulted the low fence separating the road and the park and ran through the flowers toward the confrontation.

Pol spared a quick glance to discover that the person who had asked the question was a young policeman. True to

tradition, the bobby was doing his beat armed with nothing
more than a billy club.

The man who'd had the package knocked out of his hand
froze, eyeing the policeman much as a cat eyes a bird. Politician took in the uniform from the corner of his eye but
continued to watch the enemy. The Japanese in the conservative suit smiled.

"Good afternoon, Officer. I'm afraid my associate was
somewhat hard on the flower bed in his enthusiasm to retrieve my parcel." The voice was educated and held just the
right mix of amusement and embarrassment.

The young policeman turned to Politician. "If you strike
people with that cane, I'll have to run you in. Get along
now."

Politician was in a quandary. If he tried to communicate
the difficulty to the unarmed policeman, it could be a death
sentence. Politician might survive, but not the bobby. If Pol
quietly withdrew, he could easily lose the client's money and
industrial secrets.

However, the young policeman's concentration was dis-
tracted as the four terrorists tracked through the flower bed
and zeroed in on the group. They were in no mood to fool
around and produced Webleys as they came. The copper
didn't have the sense to dive for cover.

Politician leaped, bowling the policeman over and covering the blue uniform with his own body. A hail of autofire sounded, but no bullets struck the grass near Pol and the
bobby. Politician recognized the businesslike sound of the
H&K caseless.

Pol looked around. The Japanese had scooped up the real
package and was making a broken-field run through the
park. Two of the gunmen were dead. Two others and the
terrorist who had delivered the phony package held empty
hands in the air. Lyons, McCarter, Pavlovski and Schwarz
stood in the middle of the road. Lyons held a G-11 ready to
continue the argument, given the slightest excuse. No one

had a line of fire on the fleeing Japanese. He kept the sea-side strollers in line with himself and the guns as he ran.

Pol rolled off the policeman to give pursuit, only to have his legs hooked out from under him. He fell and rolled to find that the bobby had picked up a terrorist's Webley and had him covered.

"Don't force me to shoot, sir," the policeman said politely.

If it had been a criminal, Politician might have risked it. But the conscientious policeman would shoot for his legs. Pol's flak jacket didn't protect his arms, legs or head. He glanced at the rapidly retreating figure and decided it was unlikely he'd catch the man anyway. He was really moving.

The policeman stood up and pointed the weapon at Lyons as he leaped the fence.

"I'll have to ask you to give me that weapon, sir."

Lyons looked as if he couldn't believe his ears. The policeman was green enough to take foolish risks. The knuckles on the automatic were white from tension.

"Watch out," Lyons rumbled. "You'll shoot someone by mistake."

"Set the weapon down carefully."

Gadgets and McCarter moved to flank the bobby.

"Stay where you are," he barked.

Perspiration stood on his forehead, and his hand started to shake. He suddenly realized he was surrounded by very tough customers. He had no way of knowing that each one of them would have taken a bullet without returning fire.

As the policeman fumbled for his whistle, a small Oriental with a bundle of laundry trudged straight at the tense group. Just as the whistle reached his lips, the automatic was knocked up into the air. A small hand with a strong grip squeezed an area behind his elbow, paralyzing the gun hand. Before the bobby could let go of his whistle and grab for the automatic with his left hand, Politician plucked the weapon from his grip.

"I'm sorry, but we got to run," Politician told him as he shrugged out of the grimy coat and cap.

The four men, the woman and the young Oriental took off, sprinting the length of the park. When the bobby tried to run after them, he quickly realized he'd be better off alerting his superiors and calling for backup.

By the time Able Team reached the end of the park, there was no sign of the Japanese with the money and disks. Babette doubled back for Isaac while the rest found two taxis.

"What now?" McCarter asked.

"Back to London and hope he shows up at their office once more," Lyons answered.

"And if they don't show?"

"We've blown it. The chopper's waiting. At least we'll beat him there."

In the park the conscientious young policeman guarded the three surviving terrorists while he waited for backup. Carefully he memorized descriptions while they were still fresh in his mind.

McCarter, Lao Ti and Schwarz were lying on their backs on the carpet in Isaac's office. Babette and Politician leaned back in chairs. Isaac sat calmly behind his desk. Lyons paced back and forth between the stretched-out bodies of his friends. The wastebasket overflowed with empty take-out cartons that had once held Chinese food.

In one corner the bugs in the terrorists' office had been patched into a speaker. If the terrorists used the office again, everyone in the room would hear what was happening. Gadgets had disabled the bugs in Isaac's office so that the group could be more comfortable. He had tested his own bugs by simply telephoning the empty office and listening to the telephone ring through the eavesdropping circuit.

"What if they don't return to the office?" Babette asked.

"We won't be able to round up the few remaining terrorists. It'll be impossible to prevent reprisals against Quartermaster Software," Lyons growled.

"But they have their payoff," Isaac protested.

"You'll lose a pile of people if we leave anyone free to take revenge."

Whatever Isaac was going to say next was cut off by the ringing of the telephone. Everyone exchanged startled glances.

Isaac picked up the handset, identified himself, then thrust the handset at Lyons, who grabbed it. "Yeah? Oh, it's you, Kurtzman. How'd you know where to find us?" Lyons rolled his eyes and told the group, "He traced us through Able Group Company," then he said into the mouthpiece, "You've got a problem there? We've got one here to finish up."

The receiver squawked some more, but Ironman didn't pay any attention. The sound of a key in a lock came over the speakers. It was followed by a click as a light switch was flipped on. Then two sounds came together as someone pulled a chair across a bare floor and began to dial a number. Absently Lyons put the handset back in its cradle, giving his entire attention to the speaker connected to the bugs in the office rented by the terrorists.

"Move it!" Lyons snapped.

The group snatched up weapons and scrambled. Isaac found himself in an empty office five seconds later. He glanced over at Gadgets's equipment to make sure it was recording, then followed the six toward the door. He heard the street door open and the stampede come to an abrupt halt.

As Isaac went through the Quartermaster foyer, he heard Inspector Quinn's pleased voice from outside the building.

"It gives me great pleasure," Quinn was telling the entire group, "to tell you you're under arrest for several murders in Eastbourne. We have a young bobby who should have no trouble identifying you."

12

Able Team, McCarter and Babette were taken from their cells in Cannon Row by police van to New Scotland Yard. In each case the message from the warder was the same: "I am to tell you you're being released. I am also not to unlock this cell until I have your word that you'll not try to escape until after you're delivered to Inspector Quinn's office."

Five of the prisoners simply promised. The only one of the six to make any return comment was the usually taciturn Lyons.

"Okay," Lyons agreed. "I want to kick his ass anyway."

Whatever fate Lyons had in store for Quinn was promptly shelved when the group was ushered into the detective's office. Quinn sat at a desk, but his presence was quickly forgotten. Hal Brognola stood in the middle of the office, glowering. His unlit cigar had been chewed down to less than an inch long.

"What the hell's going on?" Brognola demanded. "Kurtzman digs me out of a conference and tells me you've seconded one of his men for a private venture. That he needs you to take care of a problem in the U.S., but when he finally gets you on the telephone, you hang up on him. I get here and find you've left a trail of bodies over half the country. And the Yard's arrested you. I repeat, what the hell's going on?"

"How much does he know?" Lyons asked, nodding at Quinn.

"He now knows more about your operation than the President. How else do you think I pried you loose?"

Lyons shrugged. "Self-defense."

"With illegal weapons? Fat chance you'd have of proving it wasn't gang warfare."

"Had to. Stony Man wouldn't cooperate."

"Stony Man *couldn't* cooperate. The Bear made the same decision I would have. I back him one hundred percent."

Lyons looked around at his group. None of them said anything. The Ironman was left to continue his argument with Brognola. "Now we can't cooperate. If we leave things the way they are now, a lot of innocent people will die."

Quinn spoke for the first time. "No, gentlemen. You've succeeded in exporting the problem. I'm sorry I didn't let you finish your mop-up last night, but it's partly your fault. I didn't have the entire story, though I admit you gave me most of it. Mr. Isaac filled me in last night."

When he saw he had everyone's attention, Quinn continued. "Mr. Isaac sent over this recording of the telephone call you didn't wait to hear last night. It has set Mr. Isaac's mind at ease, even if Mr. Brognola finds it disturbing."

Quinn hit the playback button on a cassette recorder.

Able Team once again heard the key in the latch, the light being turned on and the telephone handset picked up. A chair scraped across the floor; apparently the terrorist had pulled it up with one hand while he had dialed with the other. This time they stood quietly and listened to the rest of the tape.

"One bug was in the telephone," Gadgets murmured. "We'll hear both ends of the conversation."

"Another legal oversight, Mr. Schwarz," Quinn said.

The telephone dialing went on long enough for everyone to know it was a long-distance call. A telephone rang twice, then a voice answered, "Central Dynamics."

"The commander's office," a male voice with a Japanese accent said.

"I beg your pardon, sir?"

"Aya Jishin, please."

"Oh! The president. Who will I say is calling?"

"Her London representative."

During the pause, Gadgets asked, "Have you slowed that down to get the phone number dialed?"

"We tried. The chair scraping covers the area code and the first two digits."

A few seconds later a voice croaked, "Who's that?"

"Yoru."

"Yes?"

"Partial success. Mostly failure."

"Explain."

The members of Able Team were exchanging puzzled glances.

"I have the package but lost all but three men in a failed attempt to eliminate the Americans." There was no doubting the nervousness of the man reporting failure.

"Not quite how it went, chum, but it sounds good," McCarter said.

There was a pause before the croaking voice spoke again. It was the first time it spoke more than two words at a time. The voice was thoughtful but carried an undercurrent of anger.

"Abandon England. We have everything we need from there and those fighters are extremely dangerous. I'm not surprised at the result. Leave no trace, but report at once to this office." The rasping voice wasted no words on the fallen.

"Jishin!" Lyons exploded.

"Immediately," said the male voice and hung up.

In the silence that followed, Blancanales, Schwarz, Lao Ti and Pavlovski all exchanged glances. Aya Jishin's involvement explained the ruthlessness of the terrorists and the choice of high-tech companies for victims. They had gone up against one of Jishin's ambitious plans before and it had been touch and go.

"She's already in the States!" Brognola exclaimed. "No wonder we have troubles. I thought she was killed in the battle at Elwood Industries."

"Ironman gave her a blast from his Konzak, but it was his last shell and the range was too great. She got away. It took us two days to stop Ironman from prowling around hunting her," Gadgets explained.

Lyons stood, his jaw muscles tensed.

Brognola turned to McCarter. "Phoenix Force needs you in Spain. It'll be shorter for you to fly direct. I'll get the rest of these derelicts back to the U.S. They have a job to finish."

McCarter gestured at Quinn with his thumb. "What about Mr. Law and Order?"

"Your weapons are registered. You can pick them up on the way out. Just move on before I think of some unanswered questions. There's plenty of them," Quinn grumbled.

McCarter grinned, gave his friends a thumbs-up and strode from the room.

Quinn looked at Able Team. "I've had a chance to talk to the young bobby who saw you shoot several men. After going over his story in detail, I'm convinced you saved the young fool's neck. Just go. Take your weapons with you. God knows I don't want to explain them to anyone."

Quinn turned his back on the group and gazed out the window at the Thames embankment until they were out of his office.

Isaac was waiting downstairs to shake everyone's hand.

"Your sister is on the way to the airport by ambulance," he told Politician. "Your company's methods may be more drastic than I expected, but the results speak for themselves."

THE SEVEN OF THEM were crowded in the small cabin of the black Rockwell T-39 Sabreliner. Every trace of Able Team, including their weapons and the extra ammunition, had been dumped on board by Scotland Yard men sent by an embarrassed Quinn.

Pol, as team medic, kept himself posted by his sister's wheelchair. Toni kept telling him not to fuss.

"We need something bigger and faster," Gadgets complained. "This souped-up bird is going to take us to Shannon, Gander and Boston before it gets us home. It flies fast enough, but all those refuelings eat up precious time. But I guess it will give us a chance to catch up on our sleep."

"In these cramped quarters?" Babette complained.

The complaining came to an end when Brognola demanded a complete report on the group's activities in England. He then delivered a briefing on the destruction of the Paul Revere Accounting Machine Company of Boston.

"The hostages who were forced to drive the terrorists from the parking lot were all killed. The only person who survived was the woman thrown from her own car. She's still in hospital with a concussion," Hal finished.

"That should have told you it was Jishin," Lyons growled.

"We're going to have fun trying to find her before she strikes again," Pol said. He sounded dejected.

"I already have the Bear putting the digits we do know through all the North American telephone books. We're also doing a search for a business called Central Dynamics. So far we've turned up a small aviation firm and a one-man advertising agency, but nothing Jishin could be using as a front. Certainly she hasn't registered the name," Hal replied.

The conversation drifted off. Even Gadgets ran out of things to say. Each checked out the weapons brought from London. After that they sat in silence or dozed.

They were seven hours into the flight and had taken off from Newfoundland when the Stony Man flying ace, Jack Grimaldi, called Brognola onto the flight deck. After two minutes on the radio, Brognola hollered for Lyons, then stepped out of the crew area to allow Lyons to take the co-pilot's seat.

"You still flying these things alone, Jack?" Lyons asked.

The Stony Man air jockey grinned at the big terror squasher. "Wouldn't trust you in anyone else's hands."

"Kurtzman's on the horn," Brognola interrupted.

Lyons slipped on the headphones and clamped the microphone to his throat.

"Yeah, Bear. You find our terrorists?"

"They found themselves. A Boston Threat Response Team has a place surrounded. Looks like the terrorists who made a hit yesterday decided on a return engagement. They've got hostages, and the Boston police would appreciate federal help. Apparently these guys are extra vicious."

"Jishin's back," Lyons told Aaron Kurtzman.

Kurtzman swore. Something he seldom did. "Vicious isn't the word for it."

Lyons asked Grimaldi, "Minutes out of Boston?"

Grimaldi fidgeted with the onboard computer. "About twenty minutes to touchdown."

Lyons returned his attention to the radio. "Where exactly is this going down, Bear?"

"High-tech Highway, right near the junction of Highways 3 and 128."

Jack Grimaldi was monitoring the conversation through his own headphones.

"Hell, that's right near Hanscom Field. We can drop in on the air force."

"Do it, Jack. Bear, have the locals pick us up. ETA twenty minutes."

Lyons took off the phones and mike and went back to brief his team. Grimaldi started his call to the air base. Brognola slipped into the copilot's seat, prepared to use whatever political muscle necessary to make things go smoothly.

CAPTAIN EDWARD ZAPPA was angry.

Who the hell were the Feds trying to waltz? He asks the Feds for help; he gets four specialists. Damn! He already had thirty-two men on the site. He needed another fifty and a dozen crack snipers.

Four bloody Feds! He wished he'd tried to handle it himself.

On top of that, he'd had to provide taxi service. Pick up the four and an observer. An observer! He spat on the parking lot when he thought about it.

Zap was raging mad. So were the rest of his team. They'd seen what the crazies in the building could do. They had to sit outside in the cold while the crazies held guns on the hostages inside.

It had been pure luck that the terrorists had been trapped. Zappa had felt they were slow getting to Paul Revere Accounting Machines yesterday. He'd had his men in the vans, practicing quick loading and fast driving, when the call had come in.

Even the telephone call had been a fluke. An employee had been talking to someone in a building across the highway when the lines had been cut. That someone had looked out the window and seen armed men storm the building.

So now Zap's Threat Response Team had the terrorists bottled. The telephones would be reconnected any moment. Then the negotiations would begin.

Zap wanted to pick up his Galil and march in firing, but his team would be blamed for the deaths of the innocent. It didn't matter that they were as good as dead anyway. These crazies had no intention of leaving witnesses.

Zap slammed the hood of his car with his fist. His men were careful not to look around. They didn't have to look to know that Zap's car had another dent in the hood. They didn't care. They respected Zap because he cared. He cared about the victims. He cared about his men.

The building was like most in the industrial park. One story, steel frame and sheet-steel walls. A flat roof sealed with tar and gravel. Windows were minimal, just enough to provide some light in case of power failure. They were high and small to discourage vandals and thieves.

It would be easy to hose the place with autofire right through the walls. That was the police's only ace. The terrorists had to have living hostages or they were dead meat.

There were open driveways and lawn on three sides of the hostage building, while only four feet separated it from the structure on the fourth side. His men were evacuating that building now. After that it was stalemate. They couldn't come out, and he didn't dare take his men in.

A fatigue-clad squad leader ambled up. He wore his cap backward.

"Phone's hooked up to our mobile unit, Captain."

"Can they phone out or anyone else phone in?"

"No, sir."

"Good. We haven't talked to them since they almost walked out into our arms. They should be in a panic by now."

Zappa heard a siren approaching. "That'll be the Feds. I'll see if they have any bright ideas."

He wasn't prepared for the group that emerged from the cruiser. What sort of a joke was this? He stood and stared as three men and two women climbed out. The driver saw his captain turning red and shrugged apologetically.

The men were dressed like fashion plates, except their obviously new suits were stained and torn. The tall woman looked like a model out for a luncheon with her agent. The short one would only be in the way. Each carried a sports bag with Celtics on the side.

"Who the hell are these?" Zappa roared at the driver.

A tall blond man strode over and stared Zappa up and down as if he were measuring him for a coffin.

"I'm the specialist. Who's asking?"

There was no hand offered. No friendship.

"Captain Edward Zappa, Threat Response Team. We've just patched the telephone lines into our mobile unit. Do you want to talk to the subjects?"

"The what?"

"The subjects. The hostage-takers. I was about to start negotiating."

"Don't."

"What do you mean?"

"You don't negotiate with scum like that. You get one of them on the line, he'll tell you what to do. If you don't, they'll start blowing people away."

"They all threaten to do that."

"This crew lets its leader do the threatening."

"How do you know who's in there?"

"I don't. It's an eighty percent guess." The big dude said it as coldly as if he were talking about a two-dollar bet at the track.

"We can't operate on guesses."

"You don't have to."

While the big man talked, he pulled an H&K caseless from his sports bag and primed it with two plastic sticks of caseless ammo. He stuck another six sticks and two spare clips for some sort of big gun into his jacket pocket. The other four were making similar preparations.

"What do you mean we don't have to guess? What do you think you're going to do with those things?"

"Typical cop. Do nothing but ask questions. I'm preparing to stay alive. We don't have to guess, because if this is Jishin's group, there's a reserve force due to move in any second."

"Jishin?"

"Yeah. As in Japanese earthquake. You better protect your perimeter."

"Listen, nut. I'm still in charge here. Let's see your credentials."

The blond man patted the G-11.

"I don't want any part of you. I'm not turning over authority and I'm going by the book. Understood?"

"You do that. Seeing you're too stupid to keep your butt from getting shot off, we'll protect your perimeter."

He didn't wait for permission but strode off yelling, "Okay, guys, watch their backs. They're going to play it by their books."

A brown-haired man responded with, "I told you, cops these days study only medieval lit."

Zappa had no more time to waste on the nuts. He'd disarm them and send them packing later. He hurried to the van with the communications gear.

Climbing into the rear passenger seat, he told his team's electronics specialist, "Let's talk to these creeps. They couldn't be any worse than what the government sent."

The phone rang twice before it was picked up.

"What do you want?" a voice with a heavy East European accent demanded.

"We'd like to get the innocent people out of there unhurt."

"The what?"

"Innocent people."

"No speak them people. Down with the U.S.A."

The telephone was slammed in Zappa's ear.

"What do they want, Captain?"

"For us to go away."

"What?"

"Their spokesman doesn't speak English. Sounds Slavic. Who've we got?"

Before the tech managed an answer, bullets stitched the van, and both men dived for the floor. Suddenly the place sounded like the set of a World War II movie.

Zappa dived out of the van and rolled, just as another line of autofire burst the glass from the door. He clawed the Police Special from his belt, cursing himself for leaving his Galil in his car.

The Fed had been right! Fatigue-clad terrorists were attacking them from the open side of the building. They were armed with M-16s and grenade launchers.

A police car jumped into the air and turned over, burning.

There was an explosion on the far side of the building. A minute later there was another. Zappa had no time to investigate. He belly-crawled to his car. He wanted his Galil, and he wanted it before he or his car got blown to hell.

He snatched the Galil and rolled to one side. It was only then that he realized the shooting was coming from farther away.

POL HAD BEEN THE FIRST to spot the terrorists closing in. They came in two delivery vans with the motors wailing like banshees.

He took out the tire of the first with a longer burst than necessary. He wanted to make sure the rest of the team heard the action going down, because he didn't have time to use the radio.

The van swerved and sheared a concrete telephone pole. The driver survived, but the terrorist riding shotgun was blinded by the windshield as his head flew through it. Amid curses and screams, men in fatigues carrying M-16s poured out the back.

The second van swerved around the wreck and bore down on Pol. He leaped to the side of the road, his boot scraped by the passing van, then rolled to the ditch as .223 tumblers played ricochet along the road.

The second van had almost made it to the police cordon when a brown-haired man, with a bushy mustache, and a small Oriental came running from opposite directions. The driver dived from the van while it was still moving, shouting at his fellow killers to do the same.

Lao squatted low and sent short bursts of death toward the scattering troops. She managed to kill three, but another six found cover in the ditches on either side of the road.

Lao rolled behind a metal trash dumper as autofire started to seek her out.

Gadgets charged on, laying down covering fire to prevent the terrorists from closing in on Politician. Schwarz managed to reach a building corner that allowed him to sweep over Pol's position.

Three of the terrorists opened up with a steady blast of HE grenades from their concealed position in the ditch. The grenades found a police car, then started to bombard the police position on one side of the besieged building.

Ironman did a long end run from the far side of the building. He took the long way around, coming up on the terrorist position from behind. His 4.7 mm showers brought answering splashes of red from the terrorists. One of them shouted something in a foreign language, and the grenades stopped blasting the police position and started to seek Lyons.

The vans had each held about ten Russian-trained killers. The survivors fought a careful retreat. Able Team kept a skirmish line going, forcing them back. Three would lay covering fire as the fourth sprinted to new cover. They were pressing the eight terrorists hard.

Suddenly an H&K caseless poked its flat snout over the top of a one-story, flat-roofed building immediately behind the terrorist position. Babette lined up each short burst carefully, killing three before the rest were out of range.

The terrorist reinforcements were in full flight when Lyons called Able Team back from the chase.

Babette did a backflip into the soft grass, remaining on her feet, and joined the Able Team warriors, who were trotting back toward the hostage building.

"Good going," Gadgets told her.

She nodded and asked, "Why not chase?"

"It could be a feint. We should cut back in case more reinforcements arrive from another direction," Gadgets explained. "It's always a mistake to be drawn too far from the main target."

The police were milling around and tending to their wounded when the Stony Man warriors returned. Zappa stopped his consultation with team leaders and waved the team over.

"I—" he began.

Politician cut him off. "You played the hand as you saw it."

Zappa shut his mouth with a snap and nodded. Then he said, "Doesn't make losing any easier."

"What happened?"

"You hear a couple of explosions from the other side of the building?"

"So?" Lyons asked.

"So look."

Zappa led them around the building where the hostages had been held. An eight-foot hole had been blasted in the thin metal wall. A similar hole had been blasted into the next building.

Zappa reported, in a voice heavy with defeat, "Everyone in the computer place is dead. The only good thing is we evacuated the delivery place next door. The terrorists got away in a couple of courier vans."

"You got an APB out?" Lyons asked.

"Of course. Want to quote me odds?"

Lyons shook his head. "Nine or ten more dead the other way. We're okay. How'd your team do?"

"Couple of injuries from flying debris. Thanks to you five, not much else. But this—" he gestured to the torn building full of dead "—this makes me sick."

All the members of Able Team could do was nod.

"I'll get you rides back to the air base. I hope they got what they wanted. I can't stand the thought that this might happen again."

"It will," Lyons told him. "That's what they're here for. Bulgarian Shiites going straight to glory in a holy war. I don't know who fired them up, but the woman who leads them has tried this before."

"Tried what?"

"Wiping out our entire computer industry."

"That's impossible."

Lyons wearily waved his hand at the devastation. "Are you sure? These men want to be killed. How do you stop that type?"

13

Hal Brognola stepped into the Stony Man rec room, then paused to watch the five warriors work out.

Lyons stood with his back to Politician, Lao, Gadgets and Babette.

Gadgets nodded, and the four moved quietly in on the Able Team leader, staying out of his line of vision. Gadgets's foot suddenly kicked out, caught Lyons on the ass and slammed him forward so that his face smashed into the wall.

Lyons pried himself off the wall, then slammed his fist into it, smashing paneling.

"The replacement comes out of your next check," Brognola said in a dry voice.

"I had no sense of where you were," Lyons shouted at the others. "This chi thing's a damn fake."

"It might help if you relaxed," Lao observed in a matter-of-fact voice.

"I've got some news," Brognola announced.

Lyons whirled on him. "You've finally found Central Dynamics?"

"No, but—"

"To hell with you. Go back to work. We're training."

Brognola ignored him and reported to Politician.

"Just got word from the hospital in St. Paul. The trip certainly didn't do Toni any permanent damage. They figure she'll be released tomorrow."

Blancanales grinned and said, "I'll talk to the doctor. The moment they let her loose, she'll be back at work. If he can stall for a few days, it'll be easier on all of us."

Lyons came and stood nearby, waiting impatiently. As soon as Pol was finished speaking, Lyons leaned forward until his face was only four inches from Brognola's.

"What the hell do you mean you don't know where Jishin is? You've had three bloody days. We have a company name and part of a telephone number. We're certain she has her fanatic killers in this part of the country. I want an address. I want it now!"

"You'll get it the moment we get it. Kurtzman already checked every listing with those last digits. None are Central Dynamics."

"What do you mean, 'None are Central Dynamics'? They have a telephone. We have part of the number."

"Put a button on it, Lyons! The terrorists seem to have played it smart. They took the telephone under one name and answer with another. That keeps them off the telephone system lists."

"Well, how many of them are new listings?"

"None. Chew on that for a while."

Lyons's other fist smashed out a piece of paneling.

"The longer we sit around, the more people die," he growled.

"I do have a suggestion," Brognola said in a mild voice.

Lyons spun back and glared at the head Fed, willing him to continue.

"We can set up some bait Jishin can't resist."

"Such as?"

"Me."

"You think she's after your bod?" Gadgets asked.

"A little publicity saying the man who put Elwood Industries back on its feet is leaving and taking the plans for a new-generation computer should do it."

"Yeah. It might," Lyons agreed. "She did the last raid just to get a Cray. She seems to be collecting the latest technology for her Communist masters."

Brognola showed surprise. "You think it's a good idea?"

Lyons nodded. "Why shouldn't I?"

"I didn't think you were in a mood to agree with anyone."

"I'm not. It's still a good idea. Do it."

Lyons slammed his fist at the paneling once more, but this time it didn't go through.

"Enough training for now," he told the group.

Lyons was holding his fist with the other hand.

ABLE TEAM WAS RELAXING after lunch when Brognola looked them up. The three members, Lao and Babette were sitting around the staff lounge, drinking beer and talking weapons. But they were not in good spirits. Even the argument was halfhearted.

Brognola stood in the doorway, listening. From what he could gather, Lao and Gadgets had been impressed by the G-11s. Politician and Ironman didn't like them.

"It has no ride, it's light, accurate as hell and holds a hundred rounds," Gadgets said, summing up his arguments.

Ironman snorted. "A hundred rounds. So does an automatic BB gun. Who ever took 4.7 mm seriously?"

"About twenty of Jishin's pet Muslims," Lao said in a quiet voice.

"I want more punch."

"And I want my grenade launcher," Politician added.

"I don't get it," Brognola said from the doorway. "Each of you always takes whatever he thinks fits the mission best. Why the argument?"

Lyons shrugged. "Why not?"

Brognola decided a change of subject would help.

"Everything's arranged," he announced. "The CIA has an old industrial plant in Peabody. I'll be setting up my new business there. By tomorrow the papers will know I'm moving a prototype computer in there for a demonstration next week.''

''Whoa,'' Lyons said. ''You went to the CIA? They've got more leaks than a party of drunks.''

''Yep.''

''Who's Peabody?'' Gadgets asked.

''Peabody's a town just west of Salem. It's across the Danvers River and Inlet from Danvers itself. Both towns have drives on for high-tech industry.''

''And?'' Lyons prompted.

''And I knew the CIA had acquired the building under the criminal appropriations legislation—''

''The what?'' Gadgets interrupted.

''Legislation that allows law-enforcement agencies to possess and use things taken from criminals,'' Lyons snapped. ''Stop interrupting.''

''How does that apply to the CIA?'' Gadgets persisted. ''They have no enforcement duties, especially inside the country.''

''When has that stopped them?'' Lyons answered. He nodded for Brognola to continue.

''So I had a lawyer offer them a big rent for a temporary home for a new company, and they took it. My name and Stony Man's never came into the deal,'' Brognola finished in a hurry before he could be interrupted again.

''So they don't know it's for Stony Man?'' Lyons checked.

''Can't see how they could.''

''So the leaks will just report it as leased to a new high-tech company. Clever!'' Politician said.

''It certainly is,'' Brognola agreed with a smile.

''What happens when they check with Elwood Industries?'' Gadgets asked.

''I talked to the CEO there. He'll see that the story is authenticated. In fact, he's the one who's going to leak the story of my defection to the press.''

"Might work," Lyons conceded. "Let's go look at our new trap. How about ordering us a chopper?"

"One's already on the way," Brognola told him.

THE SUN WAS ALREADY SETTING by the time the Sikorsky S-70 touched down in the vacant field next to the deserted factory. The six passengers ran out from under the fifty-four-foot rotors and started to examine the site.

"Why a factory in the middle of nowhere?" Babette asked.

"Not really nowhere," Brognola explained. "Peabody's just over that hill to the east. Someone managed to get the zoning changed and built this place, saying it would soon be an industrial park. They didn't seem too concerned that no one else would build here.

"Turned out they were storing illegal arms for terrorists. The CIA learned about it through Central America. It was their bust, and they claimed the building."

"I could practically hold the place myself from that flat two-story roof," Babette mused.

"You're not in this one," Gadgets told her.

She turned to Lyons, who said, "Don't look at me. You're not paid to risk your neck as a clay pigeon. No go on this one."

"Shit. I take my vacation with you and you won't let me join in the real fun."

"You had enough real fun in England," Gadgets told her. She dropped the subject.

"Okay," Lyons conceded. "Start the publicity rolling. Get enough bodies coming and going to make the place look used. Then set the army around it during the day. Special maneuvers or something."

Brognola raised an eyebrow. "The army?"

"Enough to discourage them."

"Oh, great! I bust my ass getting this factory and you want to keep the terrorists away."

"During the day," Lyons said. "We'll be the night watchmen. That way there'll be no workers here."

Brognola stroked his chin. The thinking seemed sound, but was Lyons losing his confidence?

JISHIN ASSUMED a deep-horse stance in front of the three cinder blocks. The blocks were piled one on top of the other at the north end of the training room. It would have been the shipping room if Central Dynamics of Danvers had produced anything to ship.

The Japanese martial artist and terrorist leader looked as if she were sitting on an invisible horse whose stirrups were far too short

In a semicircle facing her stood Bulgarian Shiites. There were forty-seven of them in two rows, standing impassively. Usually Yoru taught them the hard-style karate. They paid attention to him. But this was a woman, unworthy of a good Muslim's notice.

"You, translate," she commanded the one who spoke the best English.

Unwilling to be humiliated into translating for a woman, the Shiite looked at a corner of the ceiling and pretended not to hear.

Jishin pushed herself upright and walked toward the man, who continued to ignore her. She walked on her heels and toes, her knees still partly bent. When she was eighteen inches from the Muslim, she again went into her deep-horse stance, her fists at her hips.

Two of the men snickered.

So quickly that many didn't see her hand move, Jishin's left fist smashed into the translator's chest. It sounded like a mallet hitting. The breaking of ribs and chest bones sounded loud in the still room. The man fell back into the two rows behind him.

Those who were bowled over stood up again. The terrorist who thought he could ignore Jishin lay dead at their feet.

They drew back a step, exchanging glances that shouted of mutiny.

Before there was a consensus, Jishin leaped high in the air and came down by the cinder blocks. Her deformed left fist swung down, smashing all three blocks.

She straightened slowly and pointed at another man.

"Translate," she commanded in her harsh croak.

He translated.

"You see what you will do as if it were done," she told the terrorists.

They nodded their heads, but she could tell they really hadn't grasped the idea. The last time, she had made a fighting force out of insane, unemployed Americans, and she'd come close to succeeding. But these religious zealots were beyond her reach. Their minds were too inflexible to learn.

Jishin was relieved when Yoru returned. She straightened and waved the class away, pretending not to notice when they bowed to Yoru and not to herself.

Yoru barked something at them in their own language before they thought to carry their dead comrade away.

"He was a good fighter," Yoru observed in Japanese. He chose a mild tone of voice, but it was obvious he wasn't pleased with the turn of events.

"He ignored me."

"He was stupid," Yoru added.

"They're all stupid. How did things go in Smyrna?"

"Three-hour delay coming into the Atlanta airport. But things went better than in London."

Jishin shrugged. "You did well enough. They wiped out thirteen more men during yesterday's raid."

"Here! How did they find us?"

"The police were lucky. I suppose they called in the specialists."

"We must be rid of them," Yoru growled.

"That's why Smyrna. They saved Elwood Industries once. They'll try to save it again. Report."

"Their security is good, but we managed to get one of our men inside by giving him references from here. He planted the bugs and tapped the telephones. Then I had him stop reporting for work. They were bound to get suspicious sooner or later. I left him with nine others monitoring the tapes."

"Good. That gives us forty-eight here, including you and me. Another ten near Atlanta. That's more than enough to eliminate these swine."

"I have more good news," Yoru said. He waved a cassette tape in front of Jishin's flattened nose.

"Will you tell me now, or will I pound it out of you?" she asked.

"The tapes were monitored just before I left. This is one you must hear."

Twenty minutes later, seated in her office, Jishin slammed the off button on a portable cassette player. She struck it too hard, breaking it so that it didn't return to the starting position. She swept the broken machine off the desk with her forearm, letting it crash to the floor.

"So they think they're going to trap me with lies about a new computer. They think I'll follow up on their plant."

She paused to spit on the floor, then said, "We'll catch them in their own trap. If that doesn't work, we'll let them walk into our trap in Atlanta. One way or another, they die.

"Here's how we'll do it."

For the next fifteen minutes Yoru listened while Jishin rattled off detailed plans as if she were dictating a letter. Then she pushed her chair back from her desk and got up.

Yoru reflected that he hadn't seen her smile before; it was a hideous experience. He shuddered.

14

Babette paced the room she shared with Gadgets at Stony Man. She felt excluded, relegated to second place since Gadgets said she wouldn't be helping them trap Jishin at the factory in Peabody.

She admitted to herself she wasn't one of the team, but then neither was Lao Ti. She didn't even want to be a member. She preferred being the best gymnastic coach in North America. But why was she so upset?

Because she hadn't been excluded before. She didn't like the experience. It made her feel less than useful. She stopped pacing and began brushing her short black hair, but after twenty strokes she threw the brush across the room.

Damn it! She was involved. She'd helped Able Team stop Jishin last time. Did they think Jishin wouldn't include Babette Pavlovski on her revenge list?

Revenge list! The idea pulled Babette up short. She sat down quietly to think about revenge.

Thinking calmly, the entire thing became obvious. Aya Jishin's Communist masters wanted the American computer industry destroyed or at least slowed down. Computers tended to eclipse the Soviet's accomplishments in other fields. But Jishin's chief motive would be revenge.

Who would she want to see destroyed? Able Team, certainly. And those who helped Able Team, plus those Able Team had helped.

Who had Able Team helped? Lao Ti and a couple of computer companies, especially Elwooᴅ Industries for a start.

Babette felt her pulse quicken as if she were about to enter an Olympic competition. Elwood Industries would definitely be on the mad woman's shit list! That was a point to watch.

Babette grabbed the sports bag she'd brought from England. The H&K and Steyr were inside, cleaned and graphited. Checking to make sure there was ample ammunition in the bag, she threw a change of clothes on top of the weapons.

Then she strapped her flat ice pick on her forearm.

She had to sit down and think things through. How would she get to Smyrna, a suburb of Atlanta, with her weapons?

"Great deeds require bold measures," she said to herself in Slovak, her native language. Then she picked up the internal telephone.

"Hello, Bear. It's Babette."

"Uh, yeah, Babette. What can I do for you?"

Babette could hear him pulling his mind away from the data base networks where he was searching for some clue to the whereabouts of Central Dynamics, Jishin's front.

"I have an errand to do," she told the computer netminder. "Gadgets says I should use a helicopter. He says to tell you only one passenger, six hundred and fifty miles."

"Okay, I'll arrange it," Kurtzman said absently, his mind still on the main problem.

"Thanks, Bear."

She hung up the telephone, then began the circuitous route that would take her to the helipad with the least chance of bumping into Able Team.

ABLE TEAM WAS on its tenth tour of the perimeter since dark. The team was spread out on each point of the compass and moving stealthily counterclockwise around the factory.

The factory, at the hub of their circle, had lights burning on the second floor. Now and then a light would go off. A little later another light would go on. Occasionally a shadow would pass a window.

Able Team paid no attention to the signs of life in the factory. They all knew it was simple electronic timers and gizmos that Gadgets and Lao had rigged to make the place look occupied. They had even arranged for four cars to be left in the parking lot overnight. Eyes were kept looking into the darkness, straining for a sign of invaders.

Gadgets was wondering where Babette had gone. She hadn't returned by duty time, so he'd had to leave without talking to her. She'd probably taken a car and gone to work out somewhere. He'd be able to talk to her in the morning. Still, it was unlike her.

His thoughts were interrupted by the soft sound of cloth rubbing against cloth. Gadgets's mind forgot Babette in a split second as he settled to earth as quietly as possible.

The night was moonless, but the stars were bright. There was a ground frost that threatened to silhouette his mottled gray combat fatigues.

The shadows that drifted by weren't bad at night patrol, but they hadn't washed the sizing from their night fatigues. The sound of cloth rubbing on cloth carried ten or fifteen yards ahead of them.

They were dragging something with them.

Gadgets reached for the communicator, clipped to the shoulder strap of his web belt. It rode on top of his left shoulder, close to his ear.

He pressed the broadcast button five times as an invasion signal, then three times to let the others know who was sending. They knew their relative positions to one another, so they'd know the approximate sector of the invasion.

Gadgets listened for reports that invaders were coming in from other sectors, but none came. He couldn't figure that. Only six to eight men had passed his position. Jishin sent in larger attacking forces than that. He scouted their back trail for a few yards but came across no one else.

By then he was far enough from the invaders to use the radio.

"Only six or eight went by here. They were pulling something along the ground. Any of you see anyone else?"

The three negative responses came in code order, Lyons, Blancanales, then Lao, who had the four-click code.

"Check them closer, Wizard," Lyons ordered, using another of Gadgets's nicknames.

"Right."

Gadgets followed the group of penetrators at an easy speed. He figured more were going to have to show up before the attack.

Suddenly, just ahead of them, he saw a flash of back blast, then heard a roar, not unlike a cannon being fired.

There were whispered comments and the sound of a cannon's breechblock, followed by another boom. A second later Gadgets heard a window shatter in the factory. As he backpedaled another shot was fired.

Still no explosions from the factory.

Gadgets hit the button on a remote switch that killed the factory lights a few at a time. The small "cannon" boomed again. Gadgets pulled back to where he could report.

"They dragged in a recoilless rifle. They've put two out of three time-delayed shells inside the building so far."

Boom!

"Make that three. I'll take them out."

"Let them go," Lyons said. "Stay out of sight."

"I hear you right, Ironman?"

"You heard me. Hang low."

One more shell went into the factory before there was a massive explosion. The delayed fuses all went off at once. The accumulated blast was enough to blow out two walls and raze the building.

From somewhere near the building someone screamed. But the screams slowly died out. Gadgets hoped Politician was faking.

The terrorists came scrambling back past him, silence abandoned. The recoilless rifle jounced behind them, pulled by two of the group and pushed by another two. Four others formed a skirmish line with M-16s at the ready.

"Where the hell did they get that sort of weapon?" Gadgets wondered.

It was a great temptation to take them out as they passed, but Gadgets knew that Lyons wouldn't have ordered him not to unless he had a plan. So he gritted his teeth and watched the Communist-trained killers fade into the night.

"WHAT DO YOU MEAN she isn't here? Where is she?" Gadgets demanded.

Brognola sat in the war room wearing a heavy bathrobe. He'd obviously been awakened from a deep sleep. He took a sip of coffee and looked at the clock. Eighteen minutes past one. There must be better ways to begin the day.

He turned to Politician. When the others failed to make sense, ask Pol.

"Would you play the entire song past me once more," Brognola asked.

"No problem," Pol said quietly. "An eight-man team of terrorists used an American-made recoilless to blast the Peabody factory to rubble. Ironman decided to let them go. So we didn't interfere with their games at all. No one's seen Babette since this morning... correction—yesterday morning. Hermann's perturbed."

"Hermann's ready to start kicking balls," Gadgets shouted. "This is supposed to be a high-security site. How can someone simply vanish?"

"They can't," Brognola said in a quiet voice. "Let's clear this one up, because it won't be hard. I imagine getting the straight story about tonight will be much harder on the patience."

Hal picked up a telephone and dialed Stony Man security.

"This is Brognola. I'm in the war room. I want yesterday's record of communication. I want it here now." He hung up without waiting for a reply.

A minute later a security man let himself through the coded-access steel door and put a logbook in front of Brognola.

The log was divided into four sections: physical movement on and off site, telephone activity, radio and other signal activity, and physical messages delivered in and out. The first section yielded the information Brognola wanted.

"Kurtzman ordered her a helicopter. The navy apparently sent their new Bell 301 to give it a test run. It lifted her off at 0953. No destination given."

"Wake Kurtzman. I want to know where she went," Gadgets said.

"No way. He's been at that computer looking six ways from Sunday for some trace of Jishin. He sleeps. My guess is he wouldn't know anything. Babette asked him for a chopper, knowing he was too busy to go around talking about it. But I'll get you your info."

Brognola went to the telephone once more. Gadgets paced the floor. Politician sat calmly and watched him. Lao and Lyons each shut their eyes, catching rest where and when they could.

Ten minutes later the head Fed put down the telephone handset and told Gadgets, "The night duty officer at Bolling tells me she was flown to Atlanta."

"Atlanta!" Gadgets exclaimed. "Shit! She's trying to cut herself a piece of the action."

Lyons opened one eye. "I'd say she's succeeding."

Gadgets tried to say something, but Brognola cut him off, asking Lyons, "Why did you let the terrorists with the recoilless walk?"

"It was a trap. If we closed on them, a bigger force would have closed on us."

"How did you figure that? We never saw anyone," Pol said.

"Jishin needs all the high-tech she can feed her masters. That's how she stays in funds. She wouldn't have blasted the place without going in unless she was sure it was a trap."

Everyone sat silently. Ironman's intuitive battle judgment had stood up to analysis again.

The silence was broken by the telephone ringing. Brognola still had his hand on the handset. He yanked it up before the first ring was completed.

"Brognola. Aaron? You're supposed to be getting some sleep. How long have you been back at work? You have!" Hal looked at Lyons and announced, "The Bear is beginning to get a trail on a Central Dynamics, but he's run into some more roadblocks."

"Tell him we're on our way," Lyons snapped.

He led the group upstairs to the computer room. Gadgets ran a close second. Lao Ti, Blancanales and Brognola were right behind them.

The computer room was one of the least attractive places in Stony Man Farm. The iron walls were painted light gray. The floor was dark red and was filled with perforations. The only piece of decoration was an embroidered sampler that stated NEVER AGAIN in black letters on a blood-red background.

Aaron Kurtzman was waiting for them in his wheelchair. He looked even more rumpled than usual. He hadn't showered or shaved in three days. His eyes were bloodshot, but he was grinning and waving a piece of paper.

"I think I finally traced the sons of bitches," he crowed triumphantly.

"How?" Lyons asked.

Kurtzman's face fell. "You don't really want to know. You just want the address so you can get going, and I don't have the address yet."

"How?" Lyons repeated.

"Credit bureaus. There was no telephone number match. No business licenses. No building permits. No post office boxes. There had to be something. You can't even fake a business without signs, stationery and that sort of thing. So I started checking credit bureaus.

"A Boston printer had a complete stationery order. He checked the company through the bureau. Must have been a big order. The credit bureau gave a 'no record' response, so the transaction doesn't show in the data base used by the member companies. I didn't find the name until I started cracking into their working base.

"Problem is, I can't get an address until I either find the printer or get someone to go down to the credit bureau and look in their paper files. Anyway the phone number matches our partial."

"Then how come we couldn't trace it that way?" Lyons asked.

"The number belongs to a travel agency. They're listed as zero credit at the credit bureau. It looks like our terrorists bought out the business and kept the number in use. I had the local police check the travel agency address, but the agency's still empty."

"But wouldn't they be in that part of Boston in order to use the same number?" Lyons asked.

"Not Boston. Danvers. Just north of Salem."

"So what now?"

"I'm about to get the police hunting for either the print shop owner or someone who can open up the credit bureau to get the address."

"No you're not," Brognola interrupted. "You're going to get some sleep. So is everyone else."

The excitement in the computer room dulled. All heads turned toward Hal Brognola, eyes demanding an explanation.

"It's nearly two in the morning," the head Fed pointed out. "If we had the address right now, I'd suggest you hold off the raid until business hours. There may be only a night person at that address. There may be no one.

"Everyone here needs sleep. You people get it. I'll lay on transportation for 0910 hours. I want you arriving fresh. And I want you seeing who you're shooting at."

"He's right," Lyons said. "We'll do what the man says."

Brognola licked his finger and made an imaginary mark on the wall.

"What are you doing?" Gadgets demanded.

"That's twice in one week Lyons has said I was right. I'm recording it for posterity."

Everyone laughed except Lyons. He turned to Kurtzman and said, "Terrific job."

Kurtzman smiled again. "Okay. I feel good about it. Now you get your six hours shut-eye, but don't wake me when you leave. I'm going to sleep for a week."

"And there's no way that place is going to be anywhere near Elwood Industries?" Gadgets asked.

"Naw. It's just a couple miles from the factory we lost," the Bear growled.

The relief showed on Gadgets's face. "Then Babette can't find more than the usual amount of trouble in Smyrna. Let's get to work."

BABETTE HAD NEITHER the access to Elwood Industries nor the know-how to sweep the place for bugs and trace them to their origin. If she was going to find Jishin before Able Team, Babette knew it would require the same kind of reasoning that had brought her to Smyrna.

She assumed the place was bugged similarly to Quartermaster Software and went hunting for logical places to station the equipment that triggered the tape recorders.

At first she considered a car or van collecting the data as it drove past. She knew that was one of Gadgets's favorite techniques. But Elwood Industries had added an eight-foot iron picket fence since the last time Jishin had raided. The fence would play havoc with any attempt to collect data while moving.

Once she decided the terrorists would use a building, as they had in London, one place made more sense than the others. It was a mini-warehousing setup.

The long building was divided into units, each with a wide roll-up door, like a long line of double garages. People rented the units and stored what they wanted in their section. Most of the units had line-of-sight on Elwood Industries.

It was the metal doors that interested Babette. They were nearly as wide as the storage spaces themselves. If the terrorists were using one of those units to store the equipment that dumped the bugs, someone would have to come in person and raise the metal door to do so.

Exercising her mind further, Babette had concluded that they wouldn't do this during normal business hours. There would be too many people around to see that the space contained nothing but some sort of electronic gizmo.

So she rented a motel room and stashed her weapons bag in case the police should catch her loitering. Then, when evening fell, she stationed herself in an empty field where she could watch the warehouse doors that faced Elwood Industries.

The rubbish-strewn field wasn't an ideal place. For one thing, it was two acres of booby traps. People had dumped cans, bottles and construction rubble in the field. But she could find no other location where she wouldn't be seen by police patrols or terrorists arriving by car or truck. She stationed herself in a clump of high weeds.

The night wore on, but little happened. As the air grew colder, Pavlovski warmed herself with isometric exercises. She didn't want to move much and attract attention.

It was nearly a quarter past two when a car pulled into the lot occupied by the self-warehousing setup. Babette began running through the field to get close enough to check her theory.

Two more cars came along the road. She threw herself flat to keep from showing up in the beam of the headlights. The cars stopped, and someone climbed out of each one and stood looking at the empty field. Babette froze, then tried to raise herself sufficiently to see inside the warehouse space as the large door rolled up.

Someone yelled in Bulgarian. Babette threw herself flat as powerful flashlights probed the field. She decided that the men on the road had been using night vision binoculars to check Elwood's night security. She'd veered up right in their line of vision.

Four men leaped from the cars and took off into the field. Pavlovski turned to run. Her ankle caught in some wire someone had thrown away. She went down hard. Before she could untangle herself, she was roughly seized and hauled to her feet.

Babette wondered if she could play dumb. Before a plan formed itself fully in her mind, a fist crashed into the back of her neck. She fought to pull together her shreds of consciousness, but they slipped away from her.

She folded into darkness.

15

Jishin was in the training space by herself, working out, when Yoru entered. Her movements were being made for her own benefit, not to impress the Muslims. Her arms and legs snapped and moved through blocks and strikes.

The exercise was designed to keep the combat motions ingrained, to improve timing and to keep the martial artist's muscles in good shape. It also increased endurance. It went on and on as Yoru stood and waited, not daring to interrupt.

Although the shipping room had been used as a training center for a very short time, it already smelled of sweat and stress. Jishin's feet slapped on the wood floor that had been laid for the purpose.

Her breath came out in explosive grunts. Sweat soaked her practice uniform. Yet each strike or kick was performed with an energy that made the heavy duck canvas snap like a whip.

Yoru had to admit her style was pure to the point of being classical. *Shotokan* karate, the hardest of the hard styles, required a profuse amount of energy. Every kick, every blow, was designed to smash through the opponent's blocks as if they weren't there. Every block was intended to break an enemy arm or leg.

When she stopped, she was puffing so hard it was several seconds before she was able to bark out the single word, "Well?"

"I have more news from Atlanta."

"Good or bad?"

"Both, I think." Yoru's voice was firm. He was a third dan black belt and had no reason to be ashamed of his own *shotokan* proficiency. But having reconciled himself to Jishin's superiority, he found a new self-respect in enforcing her reign of death and terror.

"When our men went to the Smyrna storage place to activate the tape recorders in Elwood Industries, they found one of the enemy. She was sitting in an empty field, keeping her eye on the mini-warehouse we rented. They captured her."

"The little Vietnamese bitch?"

"No. The tall one."

Jishin stopped mopping her face with a towel. She stood thinking, her movements frozen.

"Both good and bad," she decided. Her hands went back to drying her neck with the towel.

"They have caught on earlier than we had hoped, but we have one of them alive," Yoru summarized. "Do you wish her brought here?"

Jishin threw the towel over her shoulder. There was no doubt of her anxiety to have a hot shower before her muscles cooled down and stiffened.

"We move there. We can no longer afford to split our forces. Leave that idiot, Doon, here to close things down. Don't tell her where the fighters are going. It is time to set a final trap for the American warriors. As long as they are around, they will only be one step behind us—and that is far too close.

"I want everyone out of here in two hours. Arrange it. We will finish off the Americans in Atlanta. Then we will terminate the ability of the United States to make computers."

"It seems like a good plan," Yoru said tactfully. "You think Doon can handle the closedown by herself?"

Jishin thought for a moment and grinned. "Those two fanatics who keep the rest praying all the time..."

Her lieutenant nodded. He knew the two men she meant. "Leave them to help her... and to guard the place."

Yoru watched Jishin stride off. He shook his head. She was insane, but she was a tactical genius. He decided that if he had to bet on Jishin against everything the United States could throw at her, Jishin was the safer bet.

He hurried away to start the evacuation of a hundred-thousand-dollar hideout that had been useful only to bring in the Bulgarians as skilled workers. The way the woman wasted money showed she thought it a matter of no consequence to force some company to give her more.

"Yes," Yoru muttered to himself, "the odds are ours."

POLITICIAN STOPPED the rented sedan behind a parked car as a large bus and a truck passed going the other way. Lyons looked up at the tinted windows as the bus passed.

Pol spoke as he resumed driving. "Southwest part of Danvers, not far from the airport. This is Conant Street. We must be almost there. How do you want to do this, Ironman?"

"Gadgets and Lao, cover the rear exits. Don't go in until the shooting starts. Pol, you and I will walk in the front, like businessmen. See how far we get before the shit hits the fan."

Gadgets checked and chambered a round in Politician's M-16/M-203 over-under gun. He passed the weapon up front to Lyons, who slid it into his Almost Celtics bag. Lyons then put a thirty-round drum on his Konzak automatic assault shotgun and put it into the bag. The two weapons lay on top of a pile of spare clips and grenades. The bag was so full that the zipper wouldn't close.

Gadgets and Lao checked out the H&K caseless assault rifles they were carrying. Knowing that they wouldn't be going inside until the shooting started, they put on web belts, complete with spare sticks of ammunition and concussion grenades.

Politician and Lyons carried their communicators clipped to the belt of their suit pants. If no one looked closely, they'd pass as paging devices. Lao put hers in a pouch on her web belt.

Gadgets leaned out the car window with his and called Stony Man. The reception was weak, but with the new antenna on Stony Man Mountain itself, there was reception. Only when he was told there was still no word from Babette did he fasten his communicator to the shoulder strap of the web belt. Even in action, he'd hear calls to his unit.

Gadgets pretended not to notice the heavy silence. He knew the others figured he was too concerned with Babette to operate efficiently. But talking about it would reassure no one.

Politician parked the car at the rear of the building. Then he and Lyons walked back to the front door. Gadgets and Lao stayed low in the back seat until the other two were away from the car. Then they stepped out and began the search for other doors to the one-story building.

As they approached the front door of the building, Pol said to Lyons, "Wish we hadn't ruined the duds Joc fixed up for us. You would have looked like a real businessman if your clothes weren't torn and stained. Surely you could have changed?"

"I'll throw these in the washer tomorrow, if it'll make you happier," Lyons growled.

The two went inside. Politician stepped up to the small window that opened onto the office area in the front of the building. Normally there would be a combination receptionist and switchboard operator seated right by the window. Two desks stood in a space sufficient for six or seven. No one was in sight.

Lyons stood just inside the outer door with one hand in the open sports bag.

"Anyone here?" Politician shouted.

No answer.

Politician tried the door to the office area. It was locked. He kicked the wooden door just below the latch. The jamb shattered, and the door flew open.

"Thank you. We will step in," Politician told the empty office as he went through the door. He still kept his hands empty, hoping to talk his way past anyone he met. Able Team wasn't a hundred percent sure they had the right Central Dynamics, which meant they wouldn't start shooting until shot at.

The noise of the shattering door didn't get a reaction, so Politician led the way through the empty office. On the way through he pulled open drawers in both desks. The drawers were empty.

A private office stood at one side of the larger room. Politician poked his head in the door. The office was empty but showed signs of having been used recently. There were papers on the desk and a foam coffee cup smeared with lipstick.

The door that led from the office area to the back of the building was unlocked. When Pol opened it, he could hear the sounds of people working. The factory area was divided by a hallway that ran down the middle. The partitions were knocked together from two-by-fours and unpainted chipboard; they stopped halfway to the ceiling. The ceiling was nothing but an open network of steel suspension trusses that held up the slightly sloped tin roof.

Lyons closed in and tapped on Pol's shoulder, signaling him to wait. The sound seemed to come from the area left of the hallway. With a slight jump, Lyons grabbed the top of the left-hand partition and hauled himself up.

He looked over, then boosted himself to the top and stood balanced on the shaky beams. He pulled out the Konzak, then tossed Politician two clips. He waited until Pol had stuffed the flat magazines into his side jacket pockets before signaling him to go around through the door in the partition wall.

Pol walked to the doorway and stepped through. A small woman with untidy red hair stood with her back to him. She was wearing a suit that looked like a reject from a second-hand shop. Two men in fatigues were standing, glaring at her. They looked seedier than she did.

"We soldiers. No porters," one said in heavily accented English.

The other one spotted Politician and slammed his elbow into his fellow terrorist's ribs. The woman caught the action and whirled to face Politician.

She was no easier to look at from the front than from behind. She held horn-rim glasses in her left hand. She'd been chewing on the end pieces. By the look of them, she'd been chewing them for a while. Her face was freckled, and her lipstick had been smeared.

"I'm looking for Ma Jishin," Pol announced.

The two self-defined soldiers began to back toward a packing case. Pol could see two M-16s leaning against the slats of the case.

Ironman tossed Politician his weapon, then leaped from the partition to the top of the packing case. The two terrorists saw an M-16 appear in the white-haired intruder's hands. They whirled to grab their own weapons, only to find themselves face-to-face with the single, mean eye of an assault shotgun. They shifted their attention to the eyes of the man holding the gun. Those blue eyes held more menace than the gaping end of the shotgun barrel.

Lyons jammed the end of the Konzak's barrel inside the terrorist's open mouth. The other terrorist saw his chance to act and grabbed the barrel of the Konzak. Lyons's finger tightened on the trigger. The assault shotgun roared once, extending the mouth cavity out through the back of the terrorist's neck.

Lyons allowed himself to be yanked off the packing case, coming knees first into the terrorist who had grabbed the gun.

"For Allah," the man shouted as he went over backward with Lyons on his chest.

His head hit the floor with a thud. Allah was forced to accept another delivery.

"You killed them!" the woman squeaked with shock.

Two short bursts of autofire were followed by the sound of a door thrown open in the rear of the building.

"Better them than us," Lyons told her. "We were discussing Jishin."

"Who?"

"Too late to play cute," Lyons answered. The hot barrel of the Konzak nudged her thigh.

"Kill me if you want to. I wasn't told where she was going."

"You didn't say you didn't know, merely that you weren't told. And I wouldn't dream of killing you."

"You wouldn't?"

Gadgets and Lao appeared in the doorway.

"We heard a single boom," Gadgets reported.

"That's all it took."

Gadgets turned to Lao. "I told you he was just blowing his nose."

"Cut the crap and check out the building," Lyons answered. Then he turned his attention back to Doon. She seemed more curious than frightened. "Naw. Waste of time to kill you. If you don't talk, I blow your thigh off. Then I put a tourniquet on it and get you to a hospital. Let you enjoy other people's pity for the rest of your life."

Doon turned beet red from a mixture of fear and outrage.

Politician could see Lyons had instinctively found the right button to push. The woman was probably brilliant, certainly not popular. She'd received mostly pity in her life. She'd probably received pity instead of a job. Yeah, pity would be the ultimate torture for this one.

"They really didn't tell me where they were going. They wouldn't trust me with that information."

Pol watched the exchange like a hawk. At this point he would have tried to play on the slight to get her to turn on Jishin. Pol admitted to himself that the ploy would have little chance of short-term success, but contrary to appearances this sloppy young woman was tough. There wasn't much chance of a quick break anyway.

Lyons played the cards differently.

"They didn't have to tell you," Lyons said to the woman. "What's your name anyway?"

"You going to give me yours?"

Pol was amazed how sharp this woman was under pressure.

"Okay. I'm Carl Lyons. My friends call me Ironman. We don't like to be identified in this business."

"What's this business?"

"Blasting terrorists."

The blue eyes still showed more curiosity than fear. "And you intend to blast me. Otherwise you wouldn't tell me this."

Lyons shrugged. "No, but I don't expect you to believe that. Just believe that you're going to have a messy right stump if you don't stop stalling. And I do promise I'll make sure you live if I blow your leg off. All I need to do is put one of those assault rifles in your hands. Now what's your name?"

She looked at him for a few long seconds before saying in a softer voice, "Doon. Selma Doon. I don't know whether to believe you or not."

"You're thinking."

"Of course."

"Cut it out and do what you feel like."

"Huh?"

Lyons grinned at her. "Stop calculating. Start living, even if it's only for one second. Do what you *feel* like.

"Now where the hell's Jishin? My trigger finger's itchy."

She grinned at him. The nervous, awkward kid laughed at Lyons's ferocity.

"You're not going to shoot," she told him.

"Why not?"

"If you felt like it, you'd have done it by now."

Lao and Gadgets had come back unnoticed. Now Gadgets's laughter rang out.

"She's got your number, Ironman."

He shrugged and raised the shotgun. "Good game, kid. You win."

"The charter company checked back with me. They took a bus and a truck to Atlanta," she said in a sudden burst of words.

"We passed them on the way in," Gadgets groaned.

"One of you phone Brognola. Have him get a chopper here to take us to Elwood Industries."

"Phone's through there," Doon said, pointing in the direction of the office Lyons and Blancanales had passed.

Lao ran out to make the call.

"What happens to me?" Doon asked.

"You better start walking. Your prints on record?"

She shook her head.

"Then there's a good chance the cops will never make you. Beat it," Lyons told her.

"To do what?"

"To stop thinking."

She looked at him, shrugged and left the room.

"What'll happen to her?" Pol wondered.

"Let's get to the airport" was Lyons's only answer.

THE BIG SIKORSKY SET Able Team and Lao Ti down at the Atlanta Naval Air Station, four miles from Elwood Industries. Brognola's pull had been sufficient to ensure that the Navy had a rented van waiting for the team.

"Now what?" Politician asked as he wheeled the big Chevy van through the gate and onto Highway 3.

When Lyons paused to think, Lao spoke up, "The motel closest to the Elwood setup."

"No time for that now," Gadgets quipped.

He got a small, sharp elbow in the stomach for his trouble. By the time he had his breath back, Pol was wheeling the van into the Misty Morning Motel parking lot.

Lao and Lyons went in. They were back out quickly.

"She checked into unit 22. No one's seen her since then. We'll look," Lyons said.

"How'd you get the key?" Gadgets asked.

Lao grinned wickedly at Gadgets as she told him, "Babette always slips Carl her key. Says you keep falling asleep."

Gadgets held his hands up in mock surrender.

The motel room was empty, obviously unused. The H&K and Steyr were both still in the sports bag.

"Why would she have gone unarmed?" Gadgets mused.

"And in the evening?" Lyons added.

"She thought it was more likely she'd be found by police than found by the terrorists," Lao said.

"So she'd be in the open, hanging around," Lyons decided. "But what would she be watching?"

Gadgets headed for the van, throwing Babette's war bag over his shoulder. "We won't know that until we see the setup at Elwood."

The people at Elwood industries were no help. No one had seen Babette. Lao wandered around the outside of the building and fence. Then she asked Gadgets, "If you were setting up a line-of-sight pickup for bugs in Elwood, where would you put them?"

Gadgets had to walk around the site twice before answering, "On the roof at the south corner. There's one spot on the road I could make a pickup without being too obvious."

Lao thought before shaking her head. "Try something less sophisticated, like in London."

"I'd put the transmitter receiver in one of those rental warehouses across the field."

"Then that's what they did, and that's what Babette figured out," Lao told him.

Gadgets nodded slowly. "Babette would figure that out."

"So here's what we do," Lyons announced.

16

The ten terrorists who had been maintaining the surveillance of Elwood Industries strained to conceal their pride when told the commander would accompany them on that night's tape dump. After all, they were good Muslims and couldn't admit they cared about what a mere woman thought.

The three rented sedans approached the site separately. First, two bracketed the empty field and the men left the cars to check that no one was keeping the mini-warehouse under surveillance.

Five minutes later the third car drove up to their rented storage space. Two men watched the open area while the other opened up and activated the radio pulse that would order the tape recorders to transmit their contents.

Jishin climbed out of the car stationed on the road between the mini-warehousing and Elwood. One of the Bulgarians pointed to a clump of weeds in the junk-littered field. "She hide in there."

Jishin snatched his night binoculars and swept the field. "The same place someone's hiding now?" she croaked.

Unmindful of Jishin's uncertain temper, the Bulgarian terrorist snatched back his night glasses. He caught the small figure rising up to see inside the open storage area. He set the glasses on the roof of the car and took off into the field, cursing under his breath.

Jishin didn't follow. Instead, she opened the driver's door, reached in and started the car. She let it idle and straightened to watch the confrontation in the field.

When the other terrorists saw one of their comrades start into the field, they followed suit. A circle of eight terrorists quickly closed in on the weed patch. Each hunter had a Colt automatic in his hand.

That left one terrorist to trigger the dump and another to watch his back. The terrorist guarding the back of the data collector reached into a car and returned to his post, carrying an M-16.

The hunters cursed and stumbled through the littered field. One fell. Another had to do some fancy steps to keep his balance. The eight terrorists closed in until they were grouped within a sixteen-foot circle.

A fresh batch of cursing announced their failure to find anyone in the clump of weeds.

Another figure rose from the field forty yards from the group. Starlight shone on blond hair and a thick-barreled gun with a drum immediately in front of the foregrip. The figure rose only as far as his knees before the weapon began to speak.

Boom, boom, boom, boom!

An oration consisting of two hundred number two and double aught steel balls blasted pieces off all eight terrorists and persuaded them life was over.

The guard at the warehouse raced to the car and started it. But then he went back to the edge of the parking lot, M-16 ready to cover the escape of the terrorist who was collecting the data.

Near one corner of the mini-warehousing setup, an M-16 chattered happily as it played a tune on the steel sides of the building and the doors.

The terrorist who was collecting information from the bugs in Elwood Industries decided to take up sprinting instead. He zigzagged to the rented car, yelling to his guard to follow.

The guard, in an uncooperative mood, doubled up and fell to the macadam instead. His fellow terrorist dived into the idling car and burned rubber out of the warehouse lot. Another burst of .223 tumblers chewed on his taillight as he fishtailed onto the road.

Jishin had smelled trouble the moment she had spotted someone in the same place an enemy had been captured the night before. She wasted no effort trying to combat a better-placed fighting force in the dark. She rolled into the car she'd started and took off. She knew full well that none of her force in the field could be saved.

As she pulled away, she saw the guard by the warehouse fall to the ground. She saw the data collector sprint for the car and get away. Two survivors out of eleven! The Americans would pay, starting with the tall female prisoner. Her death would not be swift.

WHEN THE TERRORIST FORCE ARRIVED, Politician and Gadgets were already stationed near the small warehouse building. Gadgets sent the alert signal by clicking his communicator.

Lao gave Gadgets and Pol as much time to reposition themselves as she dared. Then she rose among the weeds until she was spotted.

One of the two guards by the warehouse took off into the field. The other ran to the car for his M-16. Gadgets waited until the man in the storage area turned back to the tapes, then charged the guard from the side. All eyes were on the field as the terrorists strove not to lose sight of the target. The guard pivoted at the last moment, but it was too late.

Gadgets plunged his Gerber into the terrorist's larynx, and the guy folded with only a slight gurgle. The Able electronic wizard picked up the M-16 and used his feet to roll the terrorist's body off the parking lot surface.

When the Bulgarian killers started into the field, Lao ducked low and belly-crawled sixteen feet into the open. She'd already cleared her retreat of debris and obstacles and managed to cover the distance in five seconds. Then she curled under her gray cape and waited, a formless blotch in a field littered with rubble.

Lyons had chosen his position carefully. He wanted maximum impact and plenty of spread from the Konzak. He chose a place where the going was especially rough, knowing it would encourage the terrorists to move around his position.

When the time came to play trumps, Lyons rose only to his knees. He wanted to shoot slightly upward to make sure the spread wouldn't include Lao Ti, who was lying flat on the ground. The Konzak bucked and roared in his hand. He didn't have to check the bodies to know it had done its job.

Gadgets waited until Ironman announced his presence. Then he ran to the terrorists' rented car and started the engine. He slapped two magnetic tracking devices onto the body and moved away from the car before the data collector could come close enough to recognize the change in personnel.

When Politician saw that the beepers were planted on the terrorists' car, he sent a burst of .223 suggestions snapping over the head of the data collector to speed things up. Gadgets took advantage of Politician's fire to fake a lead bellyache.

The goon in the warehouse must have thought it contagious, because he didn't go near Gadgets. Instead, the terrorist leaped into the car, having suddenly remembered an urgent appointment elsewhere. One other terrorist had the battle savvy to get away in another vehicle.

Lyons and Lao picked their way through the field toward the mini-warehousing setup. Politician raced for the van he'd left parked on the other side of the building. Gadgets was already fumbling with the directional receiver that would keep them homed in on the terrorists' car.

The pursuit lasted only twenty minutes.

The directional finder took Able Team into an older section of Atlanta's commercial district to a four-story, brick warehouse that had seen its best days when goods were hauled by horses. The building was too decrepit to interest even those who enjoyed preserving historic architecture. It was now boarded up, and a sign on it read, Will Build for Suitable Tenant.

Pol drove the van once around the block while Gadgets checked that the directional antenna kept pointing at the old building.

"They must have found a way to get the vehicles inside that heap," Gadgets finally said.

Ironman's only comment was, "It's due for demolition. The rodents have moved in."

Politician completed most of the loop, then drove away from the building, in case traffic was being watched. When they were out of sight of the decaying structure, he pulled to the curb.

He turned to face the others and asked, "If Babette's in there, how do we get her out?"

Lyons held his five-dollar digital watch to the van window and read it by the light of a streetlight.

"Plenty of darkness left. We go in, low profile."

"A soft probe with no layout info?" Pol asked.

"You got a better idea?" Lyons growled. "That mad woman's not going to give us time."

Clenching his hands into fists, Gadgets said nothing. Jishin was going to have her revenge for the men she'd lost tonight. Babette was there as a target for the terrorist leader's rage. It could well be too late already.

"How?" Lao asked.

Lyons was silent for ten seconds. It gave the rest of the team a prickling sensation at the base of their skulls. Lyons's decisions usually required no thought. They knew he was weighing alternatives to find a way to extend Babette's slight chances of survival.

JISHIN DEMANDED an explanation from her man the minute they pulled their cars into the old building. "How did you get out of there so fast?"

"Kahil started the car and left it running for me," the terrorist replied nervously.

"I saw him run to the car twice. Once for his rifle. Are you telling me the second time he only started the car, then went back to cover you?"

"Kahil was a noble fighter for the cause."

"Shit!" Jishin croaked. "Kahil wouldn't take time to help Allah himself if the bullets were flying."

She snatched the flashlight from the sentry and began to walk around the car. Suddenly she stopped, swore and yanked something off the fender. She came back and held it under the quaking driver's nose, shining the flashlight on it.

"Do you know what that is?"

"An evil charm?" The Bulgarian accented his question by making a sign to ward off demons.

Jishin emitted a hollow, mocking laugh. "Yes, an evil charm. Wake all the troops. We are about to be attacked." She threw the small transmitter into a corner.

The driver produced his own flashlight and hurried to obey orders.

"Have Yoru report to me at once," she yelled after him.

Then she handed the sentry back his flashlight and walked through the darkened warehouse as if she'd known it all her life.

Yoru found her organizing troops by all the doors and windows on the first two floors.

"Go around and make sure they understand that the enemy must penetrate before we open fire. Also double-check them on fire zones. I don't want these idiots shooting one another," Jishin said by way of greeting.

"Where do you wish me?" he asked.

"You go to the top floor and watch the prisoner. If we don't succeed in luring the rest of the team into the trap, we will use her for further bait. I am trusting you to see she is still alive and useful."

Yoru gave a short bow, picked up an M-16 and hastened to obey orders. He saw definite potential in what he was told to do.

BABETTE HAD NO IDEA where she was. She hadn't regained consciousness while being moved. She had a vague recollection of being carried up endless stairs, her head hanging down and banging against someone's hip with each step. Each time her head had struck it had felt as if something, or someone, inside her skull had been pounding his way out with a hammer.

There had followed an endless time in darkness, passing in and out of consciousness. She had been given water several times, but she could remember little else since being surrounded in the field.

Though her head still ached, it had cleared. The effects of the blow were lessening. Her awareness was increasing. She had no idea how long she'd been lying on dusty, bare boards in a darkened room, but at least she knew she was in a darkened room.

She heard footsteps approaching the room where she lay. She relaxed and closed her eyes. Someone entered silently and closed the door again. Whoever it was stood for a long time, listening to her breathing.

Babette used the relaxation techniques she employed before a gymnastic competition. She kept her breathing steady and relaxed her muscles one at a time. After a while, the listener moved to the corner of the room. If Babette hadn't been motionless herself, she would never have heard the movement. The only imperfection in the movement was one slight clink. Babette recognized the click of shoulder strap against rifle butt.

During the long wait that followed, Babette dozed off again.

"WE GO IN THE TOP and we go in soft," Ironman decided.

"Who stays here to cover retreat and pick off scattering rats?" Gadgets asked.

"I said soft, and I meant soft," Lyons snapped. "If they run, they'll take the bugged car and we'll trace them. If we get Babette out, we'll discuss tactics after that. But the op stays soft until either we have Babette or know she's dead. Got that?"

He didn't go on until each member of the team answered in the affirmative.

"We'll start at the roof," Lyons decided.

"Easier to work up than down," Lao reminded him.

"They know that, too. If she's alive, the chances are she's on the top floor. They won't be expecting us to start at the top."

"At least the top two floors don't have boards over the windows," Gadgets mused. "Might manage it. Where do we get rope, gaffer tape and a glass cutter?"

"You sure you need 'em?"

"Quiet this time of night."

Lyons sighed. "Find us a hardware store, Politician."

Lyons's request was simple enough to carry out. However, the hardware store had bars over the small windows and an alarm system hooked to the doors and display windows.

"I love these well-secured establishments," Gadgets commented. "Means they haven't bothered hooking the alarms to those windows. Let's try the alley."

Pol stood at the mouth of the lane and watched while the other three found a small barred window over the back door. Gadgets sighed and got down on his hands and knees under the window.

Ironman stepped on Gadgets's back and grasped the center bar. Then he walked up the wall until he was perched like a spider, two hands on the bar and a foot above and below the window.

Gadgets snapped to his feet, and he and Lao stood in the alley and waited. Lyons's thick legs began to increase their pressure against the wall. Nothing happened.

He relaxed slightly and worked both hands to one end of the bar. Again he flexed his leg muscles, straining hard. There was a slight grating sound from the bar. Lyons gave a final wrench, and the anchors popped from the brickwork. The blond warrior lost his braced position and fell headfirst toward the concrete lane.

Lao and Gadgets were braced and waiting. Each caught a shoulder and heaved. Lyons's shoulders moved up as his feet came down, and he landed on his feet.

"You better go on a diet," Gadgets told him. "I'd rather catch a falling horse."

Lyons ignored him and leaped back up, catching the bar, which was now free at the top. His weight coming down on it tore it loose at the bottom.

At the mouth of the alley, Politician began to whistle a tune. The other three members of Able Team melted into the shadows. A cruiser stopped at the curb next to Politician.

"You waiting for someone?" a policeman asked without getting out of the car.

"Yes, Officer. My ride to work is late."

"To work? At two-thirty in the morning?"

"You think the bread you get fresh at nine bakes itself?" Politician demanded in a surly voice. "Hell, I can't go out at night because I gotta go to bed right after supper. And then I get your smart lip. You wanna go bake the damn bread, then go. I'm sick of these questions every time Alphonse is late. Just wait until he gets here. That Frenchie will tell you how he likes being stopped just because we start work early. Why—''

"Okay. Okay. I was just asking," the policeman said. He pulled away before he had to learn more about the difficulties of being a baker.

Lyons materialized first and stood under the window with his hands interlocked. Lao slipped a foot into the human stirrup and hopped up, grabbing a bar with her left hand. Gadgets handed her the bar torn out of the wall. She used that to poke out the small window.

They held their breath, but there was no alarm.

Lao dropped the bar and squeezed her small form between the bars to drop inside. Soon things began to fly out the window and land at Gadgets's feet—nylon rope, rolls of duct tape and a glass cutter. A moment later Lao followed them, landing lightly on her toes.

"You leave cash?" Gadgets asked.

"One hundred bucks."

"That'll pay for the goodies and window glass. Not for putting the bar back in."

"Good," Lao answered. "We did him a favor, pointing it out."

Gadgets shrugged and followed her to the van. He couldn't find a hole in her logic.

Able Team once again approached the boarded-up warehouse. There was no sign of life, no glimmer of light from the upper windows that hadn't been boarded over.

"How are we going to get up there?" Politician asked.

"Lao," Ironman answered.

"I was afraid you'd remember my climbing experience," she murmured. But she'd already wound the nylon rope around her waist.

She took off her boots and socks and handed them to Ironman, who stuffed them in his war bag. Politician took her war bag. Gadgets already carried both his and Babette's sports bags.

Lao Ti stood against the side of the building and reached up, securing a fingerhold on the top edge of the bricks above her head. The mortar was old. In most cases the mortar was a half inch indented from the brick.

"Good thing it isn't new," she said. "The mortar would be flush. Ironman would have to punch his way in."

One set of toes found purchase. She hauled herself up until her face was even with her hands. Then she found a toehold for the second foot above the first. She let go with one hand and found a new hold above her head. After testing it, she moved the second arm up. Then she dragged her body up another foot.

She continued the slow climb, moving only one thing at a time, a hand, a foot or her body.

Lyons continued to watch from underneath. As high as the first story, he could help break her fall. After that, she'd be dead if she misjudged a hold.

Pol and Gadgets spread out to keep an eye open for police, terrorists or curious pedestrians.

Several times bits of brick or mortar rattled down the wall. Lao would reach somewhere else and try for a better hold there.

"About fifty feet to the top," Gadgets muttered to himself. "She moves an arm or something about every ten seconds, five moves to the foot." He hesitated and did a quick mental calculation. He whistled under his breath.

Lyons materialized beside him. "What is it?" he asked.

"She's going to be on that wall forty-two minutes. Will her grip last that long?"

Lyons gave Schwarz a mirthless grin. "Will your nerves last that long?"

"No way, man. I'd rather be on the wall than watching."

"Could you do it?"

"I doubt it, but I'd rather try than wait."

"Tough. Quit bellyaching when you get the hard jobs."

It took Lao ten minutes to go up the first story; eight minutes to climb the next.

"Hey," Gadgets said, "she's speeding up. She can't afford to be careless."

"Have you ever known her to be careless?" Lyons asked.

Gadgets shook his head.

"Then stow it!"

The words were sharp, bitter. They made Gadgets realize he wasn't the only one feeling the agony of the climb. Another few bits of debris rattled on the lane. Gadgets refused to look up.

"She's at the fourth floor," Lyons reported.

Gadgets glanced at his watch. Sixteen minutes. Lyons had to be making sick jokes. He glanced up. Lao sat on the edge of the roof, massaging her forearms.

"Shit," Gadgets breathed. "Never thought I'd go through that when someone else was doing the work."

Lyons stretched out another grin. This one had a touch of genuine humor in it. "You've never been an expectant father, that's all."

Gadgets shook his head. Ironman was thinking about the family that had moved on when his work had separated him from them too much. It was the first time he'd seen Lyons smile with that kind of thought. He usually put his fist through something. Or someone. Especially since Julie's death.

The rope dropped down beside Gadgets.

"You're the lightest. You're next," Lyons ordered.

Gadgets realized that at a hundred and sixty-five pounds, he *was* the lightest. And there would be nothing on the roof to tie the rope to. He took a deep breath, looked around to make sure the lane was still clear, then swarmed up the rope as if it were an Olympic event and he were going for the gold.

When he pulled himself over the top, fifty seconds later, he found Lao lying on the flat roof with her legs braced against it. Not trusting her hands to hold the rope after the climb, she'd tied the rope to herself, and to the parapet.

"You could have been pulled off the roof that way," Gadgets admonished.

"I wasn't," she answered.

Gadgets sighed, grabbed the rope, signaled for the next up and braced himself.

After a small burglary, and seeing Lao climb a brick wall, breaking in was easy. They found a corner of the roof where the rope could be tied around a vent pipe. Politician and Ironman lowered Gadgets to a fourth-floor window. When he was sure the room inside was empty, Gadgets got down to work.

He ran the glass cutter around the edge of the lower pane as close to the wood as he could manage. He then ran duct tape a quarter inch from the score made by the cutter. He filled in the center and gave himself a loop of tape for a handle. Holding on to the loop of tape, he hit the corners of the cut with the butt of his Steyr. The glass broke in two places before the entire pane came out. It didn't matter; the shards of glass remained stuck to the tape.

Gadgets signaled for more slack and climbed in through the window. He set the taped glass down carefully before checking the room. It was about fifteen by twenty feet and absolutely empty. He checked the door. Unlocked. Then he went back to the rope, gave two sharp tugs and held on to the end. One at a time the rest of the team slid in through the window.

"Wait here," Lyons ordered.

He slipped out into the pitch-dark hall. Politician and Gadgets flattened themselves on either side of the doorway and waited. Lyons returned in twenty seconds.

"Stairs at both ends of the hall. Four other doors on this floor. We'll each try one before moving down the front stairs," he whispered.

Able Team moved through the doorway. Lao chose the door farthest up the hall. She put her ear to the heavy wood, but could hear nothing. It took her three minutes to turn the knob and move the door past the latch. Then she stretched herself flat on the floor and eased it open.

She could hear at least one person breathing inside.

"Babette," Lao whispered.

There was a strange tenseness in the air, but no sound. Whoever was lying on the floor inside had stopped breathing. If it wasn't Babette, Lao knew she'd have to move fast. She belly-crawled in the direction she'd heard the breathing.

Suddenly a boot stomped down, breaking Lao's right arm.

17

When someone called her name Babette held her breath, but she knew that wasn't enough. So she doubled her legs up to her chest and waited, lying on her back. With the door left open, a minute amount of light filtered into the room. Not enough to make out the figure crawling across the floor. Not enough to see the presence in the corner of the room.

When the person in the corner leaped and came down on the one on the floor, Babette instinctively knew who her friend was. Her legs straightened with a snap, and her feet jarred against an assault rifle and sent it flying.

She then brought her knees back to her chest again. This time her legs snapped out and her feet came down to the floor. Her body came up as if pushed by a giant spring. Performing the gymnasts' snap rise was something she did every day of her life. One moment she was on her back, the next she was on her feet.

Her head protested the sudden, violent action. She ignored the pain that shot along the base of her skull.

The unseen assailant's foot stomped down on the bare floor where Babette's midsection had been only seconds earlier. Taking a step back, Babette swung to face the invisible killer. She stayed crouched, waiting for a clear indication of his position.

The difference between the average martial artist and the dedicated one is negligible when things are going well. The long, painful training shines through under adverse circumstances. The unseen attacker made an error in judgment when he decided to kill Pavlovski before finishing off Lao Ti.

Instinct cries to favor an injured area. Good martial arts training substitutes cunning for instinct. Lao Ti changed her position by rolling over her broken arm. The assailant, having missed Babette, launched a kick at the spot Lao would have been if she had rolled over her uninjured side. Lao's foot lashed out in a low sweep of the floor, catching the assailant on the ankle. He was forced to step back two heavy steps to keep his balance.

Babette zeroed in on those heavy footfalls and launched herself like a human cannonball. She knocked him into the wall, bounced off and rolled to her feet. Again she stood, crouched, ready to spring.

The assailant bounced off the wall, directing his steps toward the source of the kick that had put him off-balance. Lao took a leaf from Gadgets's book and didn't bother getting off her back. She could now locate the attacker by his breathing. She cocked her legs and waited.

Suspecting another ready foot, the killer took two steps and leaped high to come over a defensive kick and crush Lao.

A lifetime of working out had ingrained move and countermove deeply into Lao's mind. She didn't need to see to know the sound of someone launching himself in a high leap. She rolled over her injured arm once more, letting him stomp the hell out of the boards. Lao's nostrils filled with dust from the ancient plank floor.

To Babette, the two steps and leap were envisioned in terms of someone coming down on a gymnast's springboard. She visualized where the springboard was and launched herself again.

The attacker came down feet first, prepared to roll when his feet drove into a human body. Instead, two legs like cannonballs powered into the side of his legs as he was coming down. There was no way he could keep his balance, and he stumbled headfirst into a wall, cracking plaster.

Dazed and disoriented, the only thing he wanted to do was get out of the darkened room, his chosen battlefield. He rolled along the wall, not wanting to stay in a position that had been marked so clearly by his crash into the wall.

Lao rolled once more, then shot both legs out. The attacker rolled along the wall right into a double pile driver that caught him on the backs of the thighs. He stumbled forward to crash into another wall.

Babette stepped behind him and hammered her fists into his kidneys. He shoved back against the wall, driving himself into the gymnast and knocking her back two steps. He gathered the last of his resources and powered for the door like a halfback determined to gain one yard by rushing.

LYONS EXAMINED THE ROOM next to the one selected by Lao. He eased open the door and waited. No sounds. A faint scent of vinegar and spices. He crept in low and listened once more. Nothing. He made a careful exploration on his hands and knees. Discarded take-out containers littered the area, accounting for the smell. No humans present.

He paused and thought about it. It made sense. If someone were hiding out in the deserted warehouse, they'd use the two floors with windows during the day. At night, when they wanted to use lights, they'd descend to the boarded-up section. If they made sure the rooms they used were blacked out well enough, they could use dim lights down there.

His musings were cut short by the sounds of a scuffle in the next room. Lyons moved to the door, but took his time easing into the hall. Warriors don't live long by rushing toward the first noise they hear.

He eased himself around the doorway. Keeping the wall to his back, he moved sideways toward the next room and listened. He could hear Pol coming up behind him. He couldn't hear Gadgets. He never expected to hear Gadgets; the man moved very quietly. But he was sure Gadgets would be flattened against the wall on the other side of the doorway.

"I'll take it," Lyons whispered.

"It's all yours," Gadgets whispered back.

Lyons stepped into the doorway just as he heard heavy, unfamiliar footsteps break into an unsteady run toward him. He launched a straight front punch. It smashed into a chest like a mallet tenderizing steak. The short, heavy form hit the floor.

"Pol, Gadgets, were your rooms empty?" Lyons whispered. When both answered yes, he ordered, "Gadgets, your light."

Gadgets always had tools in one pocket or another. He also carried a compact one-cell flashlight. He shone it on the ceiling of the room. After a long time in nearly total darkness, it seemed like a searchlight.

Lyons took in the room at a glance. Babette was crouched on one side of the room, ready to spring. She looked like a cornered panther. Lao lay on the floor, wary, legs tensed. Her right arm looked as if it had two elbows. The stubby Japanese man at his feet had fists deformed from years of pounding all sorts of unlikely substances. Old-style *shotokan*.

"You mobile, Babette?"

She gave him a shaky smile. "Headache, but functional."

"Pol, tend to Lao's arm."

He stepped outside to let Politician through the doorway. Then he glided to the head of the stairway to hold the floor until the team was ready to move again.

Gadgets gave Babette a squeeze and handed her her bag of weapons. Then he slipped into the room with Pol and Lao.

Five minutes later the light went off in the room, and Pol came up behind Lyons.

"Find something to splint it with?" Lyons asked.

"Stiff material in one of those sports bags wound around several times. Not perfect, but the ends of the bone are meeting and not moving. Gadgets had duct tape left. It's handy stuff."

"Seems we have a floor between us and Jishin's group. We haven't attracted attention yet. We're going down and through. No more rooftop shit. Babette could get dizzy, and Lao Ti has only one arm."

"Blitz time?" Pol asked.

"Not until we have to. We'll take out as many as we can quietly. The odds aren't good. They know the battle-ground. We don't. Gadgets."

"Yo."

"Check out the next floor."

Gadgets disappeared into the blackness.

Both Pol and Gadgets understood the risks involved, but neither of them questioned Ironman's reasoning. It would have been easy enough to get the women to the roof by tying the rope around each one and pulling them to the top. They could have been lowered the same way.

On the other hand, fighting down flights of stairs was a great way to get your legs blown off. Fighting up was bad enough, but going down a fighter exposed his legs and body before he could see what to shoot back at.

Lyons didn't have to say Able Team was committed to battle. The rest knew it. If they simply ran across the roof, the terrorists would discover that Babette had escaped and they would beat it. More innocent people would die before Able Team caught up again with Jishin and her killers. That was more unacceptable than battling down flights of stairs.

Fifteen minutes later Gadgets rose out of the dark to whisper, "No one on third floor."

The five of them moved down the wide steps slowly, hugging the wall. Walking in the middle of the stairs would have increased the squeaking of the steps. They moved slowly, keeping more than ten feet apart. It took more than five minutes to drift down to the third floor.

When they reached the top of the next flight, Lyons whispered, "This order—Gadgets, Pol, me, Babette, Lao. No one goes down until told by the person ahead of him."

Gadgets held his H&K caseless ready, but muttered that he should have brought his silenced MAC-10. He vanished into the blackness below. Five minutes later there was a soft "Hsst" from the bottom of the flight, and Pol began his slow descent.

Only the top floor had had several rooms and a hall, having been an office area at one time in the warehouse's history. The third and second floors proved to be nothing but giant man-made caverns for storing goods.

As Pol descended to the second floor, he could feel the presence of other bodies in the huge room.

Blancanales was most of the way down when a voice barked out a question in Bulgarian. He paused, just in time for a flashlight to pin him on the stairs.

JISHIN PACED THE GROUND FLOOR, impatient and perplexed. The American specialists should have arrived a half hour ago. She didn't think they'd alert the police, but even if they had, something should have happened by now. She mentally reviewed her trap.

The only possible hole in the defenses was the roof, but that was improbable. There were no external fire escapes and no adjacent buildings permitting roof-to-roof travel. The closest building was sixteen feet away across a narrow lane.

It was most unlikely the Americans would come in from the roof, but a skilled general leaves nothing to chance. She picked up her M-16 and headed up the back stairs. Jishin had taken the time to memorize the building. It gave her an edge in the dark.

She moved silently up the stairs, pleased to find the men alert on the second floor. Things were quiet on the top floor. Her nose detected fresh air, free of the dustiness of the old building. She slowed down, moving even more cautiously.

The broken window told its own story. She didn't bother going into the room. Instead, she checked the other rooms one at a time. It wasn't difficult; all the doors had been left open. When she found Yoru's battered body, she knew there was only one explanation.

She finished checking the top floor before starting down the stairs behind her quarry. She was in a hurry, but she knew enough not to rush. Every step was tested before she put her weight on it. In a fury of controlled impatience, she reached the third floor.

Babette and Lao were standing so quietly Jishin almost plowed into them before she knew they were there. There was some light coming in the dirty windows, but the two women were standing motionless in shadow at the head of the stairwell.

Jishin raised the M-16 by the barrel and brought it whistling down on the head of the short one.

Whether Jishin had made a small noise or Lao's chi was working overtime, Jishin never knew. At the last moment the small Oriental swung her H&K G-11 up and deflected the blow. The M-16 was descending with such ferocity that the stock broke and the G-11 was knocked out of Lao's one good hand.

Jishin tried whipping the assault rifle back for another blow, one designed to crush any arm or leg that tried to block it. But Babette was already bringing her assault rifle up. So Jishin had to redirect her blow to knock Babette's rifle barrel up. It blasted a short burst into the ceiling.

Jishin followed the M-16 with a kick that caught Babette's arms and made her drop her weapon. However, Lao had recovered enough to kick the underside of Jishin's leg, forcing it to continue its upward motion and send the Japanese terrorist staggering back.

Babette leaped after her, intent on keeping Jishin off-balance. But Jishin was too fast. A sweeping round kick knocked the gymnast back into Lao. Because she had one arm taped to her side, Lao's balance was shaky. She and Babette fell to the floor.

They both rolled to their feet immediately, but Jishin had time to take another step back and grab the business end of her M-16. The barrel came whipping up, looking for someone to spit death at.

Lyons found himself between two battles. He was forced to make his decisions instantly and without full information. Able Team would be facing too wide a field of fire on the second floor. They'd have a better chance retreating.

"Retreat," he bellowed at Pol and Gadgets. Then he turned to size up the battle on the third floor.

Between the minute amount of light from the windows and the spill from the flashlight shining on Pol on the stairs, Ironman could see the situation well enough. Jishin was bringing up a weapon and could easily kill them all with a prolonged burst.

The sound of automatic weapon fire filled the floor below.

Ironman already had his fists full of assault shotgun, but before he could bring it to bear, Babette and Lao were both on their feet between him and Jishin. With a bellow of rage and frustration, Lyons dived headfirst, thrusting the Konzak forward with his right hand. He wanted to get the barrel past his own fighters in time to fire before Jishin did.

Jishin reacted instantly and as smoothly as a robot. It was clear she could gun the women, but if she did, Lyons's shotgun would spread her over the floor of the old warehouse. Instead of firing, she too thrust forward, continuing the upward sweep of her weapon. She knocked the barrel of the Konzak high enough that the blast hit the ceiling.

Jishin and Lyons collided in midair like two steam engines with throttles open wide. Babette and Lao were knocked to either side. Both Jishin and Lyons reached with free hands to grapple for the other's weapon.

"Cover the back stairs," Lyons bellowed as he strained against Jishin.

Jishin let go of her broken weapon and rolled into Lyons's body, getting her shoulder under his armpit. In the same motion she heaved, sending Lyons flying over her shoulder.

Lyons was forced to let go of the assault shotgun to pull his arm free before her grip broke it. The Konzak dropped to the floor.

Babette still had her weapon. Lao scooped up the first weapon she could find and followed Babette to the back of the building. With only one arm free, she could feel the weapon only where she grabbed it by the stock.

Babette reached the back stairs first, just as shadowy forms began to pour over floor level. A sustained burst from the G-11 sent them scrambling back down. She would have continued to the head of the stairs to hold them if Lao hadn't called her back. She stopped short, keeping her assault rifle trained on the stairwell.

When Lao caught up, she whispered, "Stay well back from the stairs."

A terrorist poked his head up and fired. Babette cut his head off. Lao grabbed her and yanked her ten feet farther over. The floor where they'd been standing erupted in splinters and .223 tumblers.

Lao slid her hand down the butt to the handgrip. It was then that she realized she hadn't scooped up an M-16.

"I've got the Konzak. Take it. Give me your H&K. I can shoot it one-handed," she told Babette.

"What about Ironman?"

"Too late to go back."

Babette slammed home a fresh clip and handed the caseless to Lao.

"I'll get an angle for you," Lao said.

Before Babette could figure out what she meant, Lao ran lightly to the head of the stairs and fired a short burst down. She was rewarded with a scream. Then she ran a curving path as more bullets erupted through the floor, seeking her position.

Babette moved softly toward the firing. When it died down, she crept to holes in the floor. By probing with her fingers in the dark, she got a general idea of the direction of fire. She lined up the Konzak, gripping the forestock hard to prevent it from rising, and fired a three-round burst along the backtrack of the terrorist bullets.

Screams and curses followed her immediately. She was already out of the area before more lead sprayed upward.

Then there was some muttering, and with shouts of "Allah be praised," a batch of killers stormed the stairs.

The first two shells knocked them back, but the fanatics behind kept coming, and the Konzak clicked on an empty clip.

18

The moment the flashlight spotlighted Politician on the steps, Gadgets raked the room with a prolonged blast from the H&K caseless. The controlled five-second sweep of the room sent fifty flesh-seekers spraying waist high over the area.

Gadgets then dived and rolled away from the stairs. He stopped in a prone firing position, ready to go after individual targets. Sweeping an area as large as the warehouse, he calculated that they would run out of bullets before they ran out of terrorists.

From the corner of his eye, Gadgets saw Politician leap from the spotlight. Gadgets's first burst took care of the man with the flashlight. However, the flashlight fell and kept burning, cutting down the absolute dark of the cavernous room.

If Politician had been alone on the stairs, he might have scampered to the third floor before the terrorists found range. With Gadgets isolated on the second floor, there was no question of immediately obeying the order to retreat. He leaped from the stairs, clearing the hot area just as half a dozen M-16s started chopping kindling.

By leaping into the shadow area by the next flight down, Politician collided with two Bulgarians who were creeping dangerously close to the fire zone in an attempt to get a clear side shot at the intruders.

Politician's M-16 with the underslung grenade launcher was in both hands. While he was still in the air he snapped the stock forward, smashing one terrorist's jaw. Pol simply collided with the other before he could bring his assault rifle around.

The terrorist and Pol collapsed in a tangle of arms, legs and weapons. The Shiite kill specialist managed to get a knee up and shove the Stony Man warrior away. He then rose on his knees and swung his M-16 to bear on Politician. Pol stayed flat on the floor and rolled toward the killer.

The terrorist expected Pol to try to escape. The first burst drilled the floor just behind Pol. Before he could bring the line of fire down to hit the rolling target, his comrades-in-gore opened up on the position they figured Pol held. The storm of .223 tumblers killed both terrorists but passed over Politician.

Politician hugged the floor as if it were the most beautiful woman in the world. Three bullets sliced the back of his jacket but were stopped by the flak jacket. Then he reached out and slid one terrorist corpse on top of the other. It wasn't much protection, but it was something. He began fishing in his case for a fresh clip and grenades.

Gadgets played his own game of tag. He'd fire at a muzzle-flash, then roll, fire at another muzzle-flash, then roll again. Each time answering fire would probe the spot his body had occupied a fraction of a second earlier.

The third time he stayed where he was and rolled into a fetal position with his back to the enemy. Heavy fire chewed up the floor on both sides of him. A half-dozen bullets plowed into his flak jacket. One bullet came from an angle and creased his arm.

Gadgets waited for the firing to subside. He'd left his bag behind with all his rolling, and he knew he had only one or two bullets left in the G-11. He pulled the Steyr from its shoulder leather and belly-crawled straight into the midst of the enemy.

WHEN HE WAS THROWN over Jishin's shoulder, Lyons reacted like a sprung trap. There was no way to prevent being thrown onto his back. The problem was to come out of it with his shoulder in one piece. He relaxed his arm and sprang to help Jishin's throw.

During Ironman's spinning flight, his Wildey dropped from its shoulder leather.

As Lyons went over he tucked, increasing the momentum of his spin. Jishin was unable to guide him to land flat on his back. Instead, he landed on his left shoulder at her feet. The momentum of his spin was such that Jishin couldn't keep her balance, and she was pulled over his body.

Rather than risk fighting Lyons on the floor where her power kick and blows would have least effect, the Japanese terrorist released her hold on Lyons's arm and rolled away. She came up on her feet, prepared to kick her nemesis into oblivion.

Lyons had managed to land without damage, but he was winded. He was minutely slower than Jishin in rising. A roundhouse kick grazed the back of his head, smashing him back to the floor.

Lyons blinked. He could no longer focus the minute amount of light that reached his eyes. His brain felt relaxed, as if he'd had one drink too many. He knew Jishin would follow the kick with a stomp to the spine. Ironman tried to roll over, but he couldn't.

It didn't seem to matter much anyway.

WHEN THE KONZAK WAS EMPTY, Babette dropped it. She backpedaled into the dimness as she reached into her bag for the Steyr.

Lao started firing three-round bursts from the other side of the advancing terrorists. The G-11 fired full-auto at six hundred rounds per minute, but three-round bursts were spit out at two thousand rounds per minute to keep the grouping small. Lao was using the faster rate to keep the barrel from wandering when she used the assault rifle with one hand.

Babette threw herself to the floor. The terrorists were almost directly between her and Lao. The gymnast yanked the Steyr clear of the bag, thumbed off the safety and started sending the terrorists 9 mm love messages.

The Bulgarians had all turned toward the three-round bursts that were thinning their numbers. They didn't notice when the Steyr began to pat them on the backs. Babette had a two-handed prone grip and chose her targets carefully.

She could tell from Lao's muzzle-flashes that Lao also had dropped to the floor. This allowed them both to shoot slightly upward to avoid shooting each other.

The terrorists were calling praises to Allah as their companions crumpled one by one. The confusion of being under fire from two directions with no place to hide was leading to panic and full-auto shooting. The M-16s climbed as terrorized gunmen held down the triggers. Two seconds later all the M-16s were empty and the bullets had passed over the heads of the two female warriors.

They calmly kept up their target shooting until they ran out of Bulgarian pigeons.

SOMEHOW IRONMAN MANAGED to roll out of the way of Jishin's stomp. Her foot seemed to be coming down in slow motion. He knew exactly where her leg was but could see nothing else.

He tried lashing out with his own leg. It didn't seem to move quickly enough, but his foot connected with Jishin's supporting leg, just behind the knee. She lost balance and was forced to tumble and roll away from him.

Lyons used the force of his kick to roll to his hands and knees. He pushed himself to his feet. It seemed to take forever.

He could hear the whish of air and snap of Jishin's fatigues as she advanced with a flurry of kicks and punches

Lyons's fists met each kick with a pile-driving punch to the shinbone. He jerked his head from side to side as fists tried to bat his head out of the park. His arm brushed the wall, but he couldn't see it.

He could hear Jishin's breath whooping as her lungs strained to pump sufficient oxygen to burn the fuel her muscles demanded. Lyons knew the next kick was aimed at his gut. He slipped to one side and punched precisely where he knew her head was.

"Die," he shouted, giving all his force to the blow.

His fist smashed bone and teeth.

A hook caught Lyons on the ear. Lyons ignored the blow and blasted another punch at the point where he sensed most of her energy. Blood splattered him on the face as the wind exploded out of Jishin's laboring lungs.

The blood didn't seem to dim Lyons's vision. He twisted as a kick came at his groin. The kick was even slower than before. It merely grazed his hip. Her massive outpouring of energy was dwindling.

Lyons suddenly began to lose his sense of where Jishin was. A blow he failed to sense hit him on the chest, but lacked the strength to break bones. It was his only clue to Jishin's location. He hammered back along the line of the punch and heard a rib crack.

He no longer dared to lose contact. He waded in, ignoring the hook that made his ears ring. Ironman kept hammering his fists into that rock-hard body ahead of him. Then it slipped away.

He stood there, dazed. He had no idea where Jishin was.

POLITICIAN MANAGED to load one of his wire-wound grenades. He launched it toward one corner of the second floor. The blast lit several forms who started a screaming chorus immediately afterward.

"The stairs!" Gadgets shouted from somewhere in the big room. The blast had illuminated men coming up from the main floor.

Pol raked the stairwell with .223s, causing more screams. Then he took time to load another grenade and launch it down the steps. It blasted pieces of terrorists from the stairs to his position.

Then Pol grabbed his bag and started to run for the rear of the building. The grenade blasts had blinded the fighters sufficiently that no one started firing at him. He bounced into one terrorist, thrust the M-16 into the goon's throat and stroked the trigger once.

When he arrived at the back stairs, Pol found a half-dozen corpses, but no live threats. He descended quietly until he was halfway to the main floor. Then he sat on the steps and played with his grenade launcher.

Gadgets used the flashes of light to guide himself to the last pockets of defenders. He circled quietly but stayed on his feet. It hadn't seemed to occur to the Shiite killers that an enemy might approach in the line of fire of another.

Gadgets fired each time there was a burst of autofire. One after another the terrorists crumpled. It was only after Politician made his dash for the back stairs that the Bulgarians realized it wasn't his bullets that were punching their tickets.

The last three whirled at once. Gadgets had picked up a fallen M-16. He gave the bullets back to the terrorists in one sweeping figure eight.

The steady booming of grenades shook the second floor. A fire was blazing on the ground level. Gadgets picked up another M-16 and sprayed the front stairs leading up from the first floor. Two survivors of Pol's blasting tumbled back down into the inferno.

Gadgets found his G-11 and bag. He recharged both the G-11 and Steyr.

Politician emerged from the back stairs. He shook his head to indicate there were no survivors at that level.

They walked silently up the back stairs to the third floor.

Babette and Lao picked up the Konzak and the two G-11s. They stepped over a pile of corpses to do it. The four were grim, silent. Flames must have spread to the second floor, because they could see across the vast room.

They found Ironman wiping blood from his face with his shirt. At his feet lay a battered body that was once Aya Jishin.

Politician put a hand on Lyons's shoulder, saying, "Let me help."

Lyons jumped.

"Pol?"

"You'll be able to see me shortly—when the swelling goes down. What happened?"

"Jishin and I had a tussle. She's gone."

Pol looked at the battered corpse.

"Only as far as your feet, Ironman."

"Huh?" Lyons stared down at Jishin through the painful slits that were his eyes.

From outside came the sound of sirens.

"We'd better scram," Gadgets suggested. "I hate being the wienie at the wienie roast."

Lyons shrugged. "Looks like we leave by the roof after all."

The five started up the stairs ahead of the flames.

"What next?" Babette asked.

Lyons took a deep breath before answering, "I think I'd like a long vacation."

For the millions who can't read
Give the Gift of Literacy

One out of five adults in North America
cannot read or write well enough
to fill out a job application
or understand the directions on a bottle of medicine.

**You can change all this by joining the fight
against illiteracy.**

For more information write to:
Contact, Box 81826, Lincoln, Neb. 68501
In the United States, call toll free: 800-228-3225

**The only degree you need
is a degree of caring**

"This ad made possible with the cooperation of the Coalition for Literacy and the Ad Council."
Give the Gift of Literacy Campaign is a project of the book and periodical industry,
in partnership with Telephone Pioneers of America.

TAKE 'EM NOW

FOLDING SUNGLASSES FROM GOLD EAGLE

Mean up your act with these tough, street-smart shades. Practical, too, because they fold 3 times into a handy, zip-up polyurethane pouch that fits neatly into your pocket. Rugged metal frame. Scratch-resistant acrylic lenses. Best of all, they can be yours for only $6.99.

MAIL YOUR ORDER TODAY.

Send your name, address, and zip code, along with a check or money order for just $6.99 + .75¢ for postage and handling (for a total of $7.74) payable to Gold Eagle Reader Service. (New York and Iowa residents please add applicable sales tax.)

Remove from pouch...

unfold once...

GOLD EAGLE

Gold Eagle Reader Service
901 Fuhrmann Blvd.
P.O. Box 1396
Buffalo, N.Y. 14240-1396

unfold twice...

and they're ready to wear.

GES-1A

Offer not available in Canada.